STAN SAYS

SCOTT ROBERTSON

authorHOUSE®

AuthorHouse™
1663 Liberty Drive
Bloomington, IN 47403
www.authorhouse.com
Phone: 1 (800) 839-8640

Published by AuthorHouse 03/21/2019

ISBN: 978-1-7283-0468-7 (sc)
ISBN: 978-1-7283-0469-4 (hc)
ISBN: 978-1-7283-0467-0 (e)

Library of Congress Control Number: 2019903280

Print information available on the last page.

PROLOGUE

Just who is Stan anyway? He's the old white guy that watches over the Indian dump on the reservation, and his real name is not Stan. Why should I care? You shouldn't, but you're the one holding this book. You and Stan have several things in common. Like what? Well, you're both on this side of the grass, you both need quality food, water, air and rest to live a healthy life, you both shit between your heels, whether that's on one of the three flushing toilets in your American home, or behind a bush in a third world country.

Why should I follow Stan's advice? You shouldn't. Stan does not tell others how to live. Take a look behind you. That's another thing you and Stan have in common. There is no long line of folks hoping to pick up life skills advice from you, is there? Stan actually used this line on a DMV agent once when he was renewing his driver's license. STAN SAYS: "none of these good folks are standing in line to get life skill's advice from you"! It literally changed her personality.

So "who is Stan?" may not be the question here.

What Stan would offer is that you take a long hot bath, and relax, and open your mind to any eventualities. Once you are done, step out of the tub and dry off, but do not get dressed. Stand in front of the mirror, naked with wet, uncombed hair, and ask "who in the hell are you?"

Stan understands that the possibilities are endless. You could think that you're "special" because you're a white person in a community full of Hispanic farm workers. Or, you're a "big fish in a little pond". Stan has done some of this. He was the vice president of a multimillion dollar corporation that turned a good profit for many years. He was heavily involved in a regional chamber of commerce and served as five chairs consecutively; Treasurer, Secretary, Vice President, President, and Immediate Past President. This Chamber served a city of 100,000 and a county of 300,000. As such he lobbied politicians and federal agencies including junkets to DC. He was named the United States Polo Association (USPA) "Sportsman the Year" for the Northwest Region. He's driven fancy cars, worn fine suits, and lived in nice homes. The Mayor called his home phone on weekends to ask for favors. Stan lunched with bankers and attorneys at private country clubs.

So you may think you're hot stuff. Look closely at the dipstick in the mirror. Stan doesn't think you're special. STAN SAYS: "better to be a has-been than a never-was".

Odds are, if you're American, you're not all that great,

irreguardless of your social or economic stature. Stan would base his decision on how you treat others, ALL others, including animals. Stan is not a vegetarian. He feeds out steers and pigs to slaughter because he likes it better than store bought, and he controls what they eat. But Stan has an old scraggly ass long haired black cat named Foobie that he trusts the judgment of far more than what you think. If Foobie doesn't trust you, neither does Stan.

Stan has learned over more than sixty years that middle aged white folks are reactionary. This is not necessarily so for other races and nationalities. Americans want to be the fastest with a comeback in an argument, have the fastest draw in a gunfight, land that first punch, slap the timer the quickest in a chess tournament, swing that saber the hardest in a fencing match. Stan has learned, through yoga of all things, that it is far better to be reflective than reactive.

You can tell a lot about people, or the community, by their garbage. But you have to be careful, and reflective. Don't jump to conclusions based on what you want. Don't try to be Sherlock Holmes with your deductions. First off, "Sherlock" is fiction, untrue, make believe. Second, this was nearly two hundred years ago, and is not comparable to today's realities. When was the last time that you rode in a horse drawn buggy? With a pipe and a revolver in your pocket? Or had gas lamps in your "flat" for reading in the dark?

This book is fiction. Any reference to specific individuals are unintended, and coincidental. There are three sections; Life, Finances, and Relationships. All Rights reserved.

CONTENTS

Section Two
Finances

Section Three
Relationships

STAN SAYS:

SECTION ONE

LIFE

A: Rosie is a good example. Rosie is a young Indian woman, about twenty five years old. Every Wednesday morning she drives her black Cadillac Escalade to the dump. She is a buxom gal and pretty, if your thing is big brown women. She has a style. She wears some hoity toity sunglasses that are huge, and apparently the current in vogue style. She has fancy, tight, bleached jeans that have blingy designs embroidered on both back pockets, which she flaunts when she walks. The tight jeans have precisely located tears with frayed cotton, that show her knee high boot style that is under the jeans, just below the rear pockets, which are sashaying around. Stan has never seen her jet black hair down, but it must be waist length by the large bun rolled up on top of her head, and fastened with a trendy stick pin. Rosie is not modest about displaying her large chest. She is very gregarious, flirting, smiling and laughing with her bright white teeth between bright red lips on her dark completion.

Her upbeat behavior causes Stan to reflect. Stan knows that she is not rich, but that she devotes her modest means to her fashion and transportation. That must bring her great happiness as she is always laughing and smiling, Stan reflects that if everyone in the world were this happy in life, there would be no need for armies, nuclear weapons, drones, or police and courts. Stan does reflect on how well border protections work, or don't work, and even if they are necessary. He ponders that if all borders were just swung open, at first there would be some vast migrations, but that eventually, everyone would probably settle right back where they began. Stan ponders what wonders humans could produce if military and police budgets were diverted to humanitarian needs. He also ponders that this mass segment of employment is one of the major education systems for America.

Rosie always dumps off around one hundred dirty diapers each week. Stan reflects that if he was clearing out a hundred dirty diapers from his Cadillac that he would be joyous as well. But this Wednesday morning something is different. She has a stern demeanor, and is also tossing what appear to be fairly new Wrangler men's blue jeans, long sleeved western style shirts, a black cowboy hat, and nice cowboy boots. She still has the tight fancy jeans, worth at least one hundred dollars, and the big sunglasses, another one hundred dollars, even though it's cloudy outside. Gathered anything Sherlock?

What the horny middle aged white American male

that truly believes he is God's gift has concluded reaction-
ally to his own delusions, rather than reflectively out of
a true concern for the woman, is that Rosie is sexually
active; the diapers prove that. And she has thrown her
man out, hence tossing the good clothes', which makes
her available. Stan's dad always coached Stan's sisters "If
you're advertisin' you must be sellin'". It took Stan a while
to shake his redneck father's life skills advice.

The reality? Rosie is a virgin; "ain't had none, don't
want none". She runs a small daycare for all of her friend's
children, cash on the side. Her brother recently died when
a drunk driver crossed the centerline and head-on'ed his
car going home from church. Being trendy is a priority to
Rosie. How she looks, what she drives. Nothing could be
further from Stan's list of desires, but he does not judge
her. STAN SAYS: "if everyone in the world was just like
me, the world would be a boring place". She's not man
hunting. Quite the opposite. A few years down the road
she decides that she prefers women to men, and becomes
a lesbian, living with a girlfriend. This woman is her coworker running the day care, is very fashionable as well,
and watches the kids when Rosie goes to the dump.

Stan didn't step on it. He was reflective. He used to be
reactionary. This will come out in the relationship section,
but Stan is happily married to his true love and would do
nothing to risk their relationship. He respects his wife.
But he did have some unanswered questions; why do
Indians dress up like cowboys? He sees this almost daily.

You never see a cowboy dressed like an Indian except in the Village People dance band. And why haul diapers in your Escalade? Why not just get a dumpster? And if you are hauling dirty diapers in your Escalade, do you roll all the windows down, or leave them up and crank the AC? Stan reflected on these matters and finally just accepted them, without judgment. He has learned over time that some things just are; the sun comes up and goes down. The roosters' crow. Dogs chase cats. Some things just aren't worth fighting; you're not going to change it. Just accept it without judgment – let it go.

B: Childhood. Stan adopted this attitude at a young age. He was in his early teens. He went salmon fishing to a little town called Sekiu, on the Strait of Juan De Fuca on the Olympic Peninsula in Northwest Washington State. This is about twenty miles east of the Pacific Ocean, and about the same distance south of Canada. Stan's father's favorite television show was All in the Family starring Carroll O'Connor as Archie Bunker. Archie was Stan's dad's hero. His dad was a racist ultra-right wing belligerent sexist in his fifties, just like Archie Bunker. Stan and his dad stayed in a pick-up camper in the parking lot for boat trailers next to the marina. Mr. O'Connor was in a small rental motor home parked close to them. Both Stan and his father were very excited. The marina is a busy place at 5:00 in the morning. There's bait to cut, fuel for the boat, beer and ice in the cooler, breakfast, all sorts of activity. Stan and his dad ran across Archie Bunker several times on the trip. Stan's dad was so dejected. Archie wasn't himself. He was a kind, polite, gentlemen holding doors for folks, smiling, just a genuinely nice fellow. His wife was there, and she was not Edith! It ruined the show for his father. It was never the same. STAN SAYS: "when you do the right thing people will question your motives; do the right thing anyway".

Stan's father just could not accept the fact that Mr. O'Connor was a professional actor, and that Archie Bunker was make believe, not real. This guy looked exactly like him, but he did not behave with any similarity. Stan would come to recognize Carol O'Connor as one of the best actors he would ever see. Stan watched the show from then on. His father wouldn't. Through all of this Archie Bunker interchange experience, Stan developed a new Pearl. STAN SAYS: "It's better to be thought a fool than to speak up and remove all doubt".

Stan started working at age fourteen in a truck shop alongside his father. His mother had passed away when he was ten years old. His father never remarried. But Stan reflected that young men develop between ages ten and fifteen. If you don't have them by then, you've lost them, forever. He would recognize and confirm this later in his life. Stan's diet was pretty bland. Once he obtained his driver's license at age sixteen he started working full time in the truck shop on the swing shift and weekends. His dad worked days Monday through Saturday, so they really never spent much time together after that. Once Stan began driving at sixteen, he ate the same thing, every day, seven days a week, lunch and dinner; two cheeseburgers, a bag-o-fries, and a large Coke from Rossows U-tote-em, which was next door to the truck shop. After a couple years of that he changed to Big Johns on the other end of town because they had Pin Ball Wizard on their juke box. So for Stan, the dinners at home around the family table ended when he started driving.

Stan had to consider college. School was dead easy for Stan. Indeed he had straight A's from the seventh grade on, except for two C's in senior history, because that teacher demanded "extra" credit to get a higher grade. Stan couldn't do the "extra" work because he had a full time job after school. This teacher, Mr. Vancil, considered himself a college professor, even though he was just a history teacher in a small high school in a backwater hick town. But Stan did consider college. He had older brothers and sisters that went to college. Stan was offered some good scholarships. One was a full ride to a good school in his state. He also pursued the military, but as the war in Viet Nam had just ended, the draft was discontinued, and the military really didn't need more people. The United States discontinued registration for the draft the day before Stan's eighteenth birthday. To

Stan, the military was where the kids that didn't have any hope or ability, but they needed to leave home, went. Stan's father of course weighed in on the matter in true Archie Bunker style; "I'd rather be smart than educated". Stan is reflective now, but he wasn't back then.

Stan made as much money as folks he knew that went to college and became teachers, or other "professions", even though he was just a seventeen year old high school graduate. Stan had skipped the third grade. He went for a week or two, and then the school system moved him to the fourth grade, which everyone thought fantastic. In the end, when Stan became reflective, this was a disservice to him, because he was not as developed as the kids a year older for sports, dating, and other social affairs.

Indeed, he was under six feet tall when he graduated. At a high school basketball game a year later his coach saw him at six feet five inches, and was amazed. That one year would have made a big difference. Stan's mother passed away shortly after he began the fourth grade, so emotionally, he wasn't prepared for that much change.

So Stan never went to college. He went to work as the garbage company mechanic in the small hick town. The company was purchased by a regional company and he was transferred to a larger town. This company was union. Stan gained some of his political insight here. Boeing was a big customer, really big. To service their accounts your company had to be union. All of the haulers in the region were Teamsters, so all of the competition was also union.

But the mechanics got to choose; they could either be Teamsters, or Aerospace union as they were mechanics, not truck drivers. Stan chose the Aerospace union. This membership required continuing education that was paid for by the union. Stan enrolled at a junior college and took night classes for advance layout drafting, math, and P.E. He later reflected that had he gone to college out of high school, he could have achieved something. But Stan enjoyed hauling other people's garbage. He gathered a sense of accomplishment serving his community in this unappreciated way. Generally, the public looks down on the garbage man. Stan enjoyed the anonymity of the job. STAN SAYS: "let's not show up for a week and see if anybody notices".

C: The pissin' match. These can happen anywhere, anytime. It could be a coworker, family member, customer, cop, spouse, or neighbor. It doesn't matter. It can be in public, in the break room at work, in a vehicle, or in bed. STAN SAYS: "don't enter a battle of wits with an unarmed man". This is a time to be reflective. It is common for Americans, and particularly middle aged white males, to be reactionary; to have that quick comeback in an argument, to slap the timer the fastest in a chess tournament, to be the fastest draw in a gunfight, to swing that saber in a fencing match.

This is reflective thought control. This is not reactive thinking. Reacting only escalates the argument. Think about it. If you enter a battle of wits with someone stupid, it's a given that you'll win, right? After all, you're smarter than them and you're going to prove it!

But what if you don't win, dumbass? How embarrassing is that? To lose a battle of wits with someone that has no ammo? That's a moniker you won't lose over the Super Bowl weekend. And if you do happen to win, can you take pride in outwitting an idiot? Can you make any money, like selling tickets? There is no upside, so to repeat; STAN SAYS: "Don't enter a battle of wits with an unarmed man", there is no point, and no upside.

Rather, reflect. Just get close to the person. Make no sound, or even a heavy exhale. Adopt a relaxed posture. Make eye contact from no further than two feet away, and smile knowingly (this may take practice in front of a mirror). Not smart ass, just knowingly. They will be used to this because almost everyone is smarter than them. Then, turn and exit the area. Don't run, don't whistle, just be calm and walk away. They may yell, and even chase you. Just smile, and breathe.

Eventually they will contact you, either because they need something from you, or they want to apologize. Yes, Stan suggests that they will need something from you, because, well, in Stan's experience, stupid people are needy. If you are needy to a stupid person, you may want to reflect on your life.

D: Death. Yes, you are going to die. Stan will not tell you what to do. He feels he is only qualified to show you how not to do things by his personal experiences. But Stan will guarantee that you are going to die. What you do with his Pearls of Wisdom is up to you. Stan will discuss police services later, but the reason he has no interest in being a cop is because he doesn't want to enforce rules that require others to live a certain way. Stan has accepted mortality following a near fatal brain injury. Stan is constantly amazed at people in their late fifties, sixties, or older, that believe they will live forever. Sam knows that he will expire, and that he is one day closer than he was yesterday.

Stan's wife saved his life. They were not yet married at the time. Upon reflection Stan reckons that may be the reason why. But his wife is a seasoned ER nurse. In his hospital room in the mental lockdown ward, he had a roomy named Jack that had been hit in the head by a backhoe bucket. Stan's wife, pre-wedding, was sitting on the edge of his bed. Jack's wife was doing the same at his bed. Stan overheard Jack tell his wife "I feel like I'm going to die." Stan's pre-wife jumped up from the bed, ran to the door, stepped in the hall and yelled "crash cart!" Nurses and medical assistants came a running. Two minutes later they were pulling the bedspread over Jack's head.

Holy shit! Stan's pre-wife said "when somebody says that, call for the crash cart." There's a lesson Stan will never forget. STAN SAYS: "when they say they feel like they're going to die, get the crash cart." He has other death related Pearls. STAN SAYS: "when you're on this side of the grass, it's a good day."

Once you adopt a reflective mindset, there will be no bad days. Some days will be better than others, but if you're on this side of the grass, it can't be that bad. If someone else got the promotion or the company car, congratulate them, sincerely, eye to eye. There will be strings. It may be that you're lucky you didn't get it.

So be reflective about your death. One of Stan's concerns is leaving his wife and family any debt. He has a modest 401k. He is working past his early social security retirement date, to pay down debt, and to receive more benefits. He drives a beater pick-up with plastic taped in for the driver's side window, because he doesn't want a car payment. He has a damn fine tractor and barn, which are his priorities. His four barn cats are happy in their barn, and that brings him happiness. Stan has no clue how long he will live. His family history is all over the board. He has no health issues that he knows of. He eats and sleeps well. He's fifteen pounds overweight, but he is active. He does hot yoga on Saturday mornings.

Stan is reflective on his death. He does not fear it. He is cautious driving, operating equipment, climbing a ladder. He appreciates that it is harder to clip his toenails' now as opposed to thirty years ago, but at least he can still do his own. His grandfather was four hundred pounds at eighty four years old, and could no longer clip his own toenails. Stan's dad had to perform that duty, and dreaded it. Stan's dad was a five pack a day chain smoking alcoholic, and he died of lung cancer at age sixty nine. Stan has never smoked or used any drugs. He does not like prescription pain killers because he can't control his body. Stan feels the pain is better than the lack of body control. Stan drinks beer daily, so by many's definition, he too is an alcoholic, but Stan hasn't been drunk in twenty years.

Stan spent a lot of time around his grandfather once his mother passed away. Stan's grandmother, his dad's mom, passed away when his father was the same age as Stan, so in that way they had a connection, although it was never discussed. Stan's grandparents both emigrated through Ellis Island from Scotland fifty years before Stan was born, before World War One. They met on the boat and were married in the United States. They had three children. He was only eighteen years old. His occupation was a farmer, which in those pre-tractor days also meant a horseman. He was a huge man. At one time he had been very fit. Back in those days the Farmers Co-op had contests. Stan's grandpa was the only man that could throw a bale of hay over a train box car! He was ornery. Stan didn't know if it was the pint of whiskey and the quart of vanilla ice cream that he had every morning for breakfast, without fail, or not.

Some years later AC/DC came out with a song "long road to the top" in which they did an absolutely fantastic job of blending "the squirlin' of the pipes" to an electric guitar and drums. Stan reflected that in his youth, this would have been his grandfather, blowing bagpipes in a rock and roll band. Indeed, he would never discuss his past in Scotland. Once he passed away Stan's aunt hired a family lineage company out of Great Britain to research it and see what they could find. They could find no record of him or his family. His aunt did not understand because she had the documents from when he arrived at Ellis Island in New York.

They explained that this was common in that era; that young people were "indentured" by their poor parents, for a fee, usually for seven years, to another family as cheap labor. It was common for the indentured children to "jump ship" and travel to America to be free. They supposed that Stan's grandfather may have "jumped ship". Nothing else was ever known. Then some five years later all of Stan's brothers and sisters got an inheritance of eleven pounds from an "Uncle Tugg" in Australia. Apparently Tugg was a brother to Stan's grandfather. Australia was a penal colony where criminals were sent from Great Britain, so Stan reflects that his grandfather's family really was "bad ass". It makes the AC/DC tune relative to Stan.

So Stan is as reflective about his death, as he is everything else. It will come; there is no way around it. Of course Stan could end his own life, but he is not about to. No problem is that big. Several people that Stan knew committed suicide. Stan learned that all they do is create heartache dramas for friends and family. They caused more problems than they solved.

Stan doesn't like the macabre way that Americans perform funerals. He isn't too hot on the way the Indians do it either, but he appreciates that it is "their way". But the whole open casket looking at the person dead, sometimes touching them, sometimes "kissing" them, is just too much. STAN SAYS: "Cremate, me, dump me on the farm, throw a party, and take care of my cats". Before Stan and his wife "bought the farm" (literally), STAN SAID: "use me as ADC (alternate daily cover) at the landfill."

E: Religion. Stan has researched religion in his own way. He considers himself a Christian. He had been a member of two churches for many years, following the first two divorces. Upon reflection, he considers himself agnostic, even though he's not sure what that word means, it just sounds better than atheist. A lot of religious Christians are very zealous, and want to go to heaven, but not today! Huh?

Stan has traveled to different countries and witnessed

different religions. He was raised in a Christian community, by his father's definition; "there are more churches than taverns". So he was surrounded by Christ on a cross all of his childhood, even though his family did not attend church. As an example, his kindergarten class and his Cub Scout meetings were in church basements, The First Assembly of God, and a Catholic church. As Stan grew, and traveled, he came to understand that less than one quarter of all humans are Christian. The other three quarters of the world are Buddhist, Hindu, Muslim, Islam, Jewish, or other faiths. Can all of them be wrong, and hell bound?

As Stan gets to know the Indians more, he is drawn to their "Creator". Stan's pretty sure someone or something out there is in charge. But the Indians appreciate all life, and most are reflective. He reckons it could be that their "Creator" is actually the leader of all the various religions on earth, or even in the universe.

Stan has instructed all of his family not to waste what little money he has on any grand gestures to save his life. If he gets cancer or some other fatal disease he is willing to attempt any treatment that their insurance or Medicare will pay for, including chemotherapy, radiation, or surgeries, but do not fly him far away for some "trial" procedure. Stan wants to be cremated and dumped on his farm. His family hates it when he discusses his death. STAN SAYS: "you need to accept mortality, including mine." And "when you get out of bed in the morning, and nothing hurts, it's a good day."

So Stan won't question your religious beliefs, or lack thereof. Quite the opposite. Stan would like to hear your opinion on religion, and any "afterlife" that you may believe in. Stan won't tell you how to live, and he can't suggest how to die, because he has no firsthand experience. His wife and he have discussed this at length. As an ER nurse she had a lot of people that died in her arms. The only firsthand experience Stan has is he recalls having to decide to live or die, around the same time his lock down mental ward roomy, Jack passed. He was just lying in bed, and knew that he had to make a choice. Dying was easy, just fall asleep. Living was harder. You had pain, and had to kick yourself in the ass. Stan chose the hard way, as were most of his life experiences. But there was no "light" or tunnels, or "voices" that his wife had questioned.

F: Law and Order. Stan's career has mirrored law enforcement for over thirty years. To gain a perspective, think about your own neighborhood. How often do you see a police cruiser go past your house? Ever? How often do you see a garbage truck? Every Thursday? Fridays' after Thanksgiving, Christmas and New Year's? When it snows? When it's one hundred and ten out? Do you know your garbage man's name? He / she can tell you what strange car is not from around here, which dog bites, which can will be heavy with long neck beer or wine bottles.

Stan's experiences began when he was a night shift mechanic in a big city. The heavy routes were done at night to forgo the traffic. All of the bosses, supervisors', salesmen, customer service rep's worked days and went home at 5:00. Often the night shift mechanics handled problems or issues, as the driver had a garbage truck, and a route to do, and the mechanics had a shop truck and a telephone. It was common, a couple times a year, for a route driver to find a new born infant in the garbage dumpster. The odds were about even if it was alive or dead. The driver called into the shop via a two way radio, and the mechanic called the police precinct for that neighborhood. Relationships developed over extreme circumstances. The infants were placed in the dumpster by prostitutes that could not, or would not, care for the child. If the infant was alive, often the child was already a crack addict.

Stan would meet the police at the site, and the infant would either go to Child Protective Services and a hospital, or the morgue. The police would take a report. The driver didn't know anything. If the infant was alive, the crying probably alerted the driver. Stan reflected that a lot of dead babies were probably never found. But the police always wanted to impound the truck as evidence in a murder investigation. Stan would find himself arguing law, which was a far cry from changing oil or greasing a garbage truck. The Company couldn't be down a truck, often times for several months, so Stan would offer to let them take the dumpster, and he would exchange it out. The truck had nothing to do with the murder. It had not even contacted the dumpster yet.

In this same job he became a sort of gang expert. All of their dumpsters were graffiti'ed. There were a lot of different designs and words. There were a lot of graffiti laws passed to attempt to curb the problem. STAN SAYS: "an arrest is not a conviction, and a judgment is not payment". But the garbage company ended up creating a full time job repainting the dumpsters, so in that regard it was economic development in a way.

Stan just rigged up a portable spray rig, and placed cardboard on the ground around the container, and painted it. This saved a lot of time and expense exchanging the container, and taking it back to the shop. This container painting was actually against the law because the overspray was not filtered, but the paint police don't watch the dumpsters in the back alley at midnight. It was common, in a day or two, to have to paint the container again. It would be re-covered with graffiti. Stan ran across the same police that investigated the infant murders. Stan showed them which dumpster had the new aerosol cans in it. A kid that worked in the store threw the cans in the dumpster, and a sidekick outside then dug them out before the truck dumped the container. The police and city council had assumed this was shoplifting, and passed laws to lock the paint in cabinets in the store. The "inside man" (kid) was not stealing them out of their locked cabinets, he was just grabbing cases as the paint was delivered in the back room, and simply threw the whole box in the dumpster. This explained why the color was so consistent at certain times. Again, all the powers that be considered it gang colors, like the Nortega's and Sorento's in LA.

STAN SAYS: "You can't tell the gang by the colors". Actually, there were no gangs. The organized gang's had better things to do than paint dumpsters in back alleys that nobody would see. Besides, they were afraid of the rats, which were cat sized. The taggers were about an even split, boys and girls. He got to know several as they taunted him that they would retag the dumpster, and some even offered to take requests. Some enjoyed painting so much that Stan let them paint the dumpsters.

The boys tended to be loners between sixteen and twenty that rode freight trains from as far away as New York, Chicago, and Houston. They usually sprayed their street name, often on box cars that roamed from town to town. They had usually got sick of home, or had been abused. There were seventeen girl "gangs" in this city. Stan could tell the girls marks just like a girls handwriting. These "gangs" usually didn't have a formal structure or leader. As often as not the leader that day was whichever one had stolen a car, or conned a mark out of a hundred bucks. These girls were usually fourteen to eighteen, and found safety in their numbers as opposed to being abused at home. These sad human interactions are a part of Stan's reflection. These poor kids didn't know where their next meal would come from, may be a dumpster, or where they would sleep tonight. They usually slept during the day, often in a dumpster, and prowled at night. When they got desperate they could just get arrested or go to the ER for a dry bed, shower, and a meal. But almost always, they were happy and upbeat. Their current situation was much improved compared to whatever they had escaped.

Stan learned a lot about drugs, even though he never used any. He came to understand that the Nazi's had developed methamphetamine for their planned invasion of Russia. The orders were to make a drug that would give the soldiers a feeling of invincibility so that they could fight maniacally with no food or sleep for two or three days. It must be brewed from chemicals available in the motor pool. They must be able to cook it in their helmets. The side effects were not a concern. They recognized that these soldiers would be killed soon anyway.

When most folks think of meth manufacturers the urban myth is that it's hippies in trailers out in the woods. That may have been the case twenty years ago. Stan knew, from the chemical containers in the dumpsters, that nowadays they cook meth in a motel room, and simply drive away. As often as not the maid is a foreigner that speaks no English, reads no language, has no training, and she simply cleans the room with no regard to the chemical byproduct dangers.

Stan sees a lot crime. The lowest paid person at a business is the night janitor, who, what else, takes the trash out. They often steal merchandise, throw it in the dumpster, and a sidekick collects it before the truck gets there to dump the container. Often, these items are returned by the sidekick for a cash "refund".

Of course the DEA and other law enforcement agencies are switched on to these circumstances, even if the business owners are not. The DEA actually allows federal "law enforcement" folks to volunteer for assignments for undercover work. These task forces often want to go through a trash can or dumpster to track receipts for materials, power bills, phone bills, etc. The reason they accept volunteers is because they want total strangers to a given region to avoid recognition and detection.

So Stan gets these undercover agents to ride in an empty garbage truck with him to cycle into a route, pick up the trash separately, and take it back to the shop to dig through it. These are Navy submarine M.P.'s, Forest Service Park Rangers, Secret Service agents, Immigration; generally they have no spouse or children, and frankly, are kids themselves. As often as not they got their garbage man insight from the "Men at Work" movie. Stan made them change into a company uniform and lose the red bandana. Stan usually drove the second route truck himself because; one, they were armed, and Stan didn't want any of his drivers caught in a shootout, and two, Stan has been around the block enough to know that the circumstance may involve his driver. STAN SAYS: "just when you think you've seen it all, you get a surprise".

The Indian law enforcement has its own interesting conundrums. Of course, people are people. But first off, everyone in the Tribe is related, at least as an in-law or a second cousin. This includes the cop, the prosecuting attorney, and the judge. Next is that not everyone on the reservation is an Indian. In fact only about one quarter of the population of the reservation Stan runs the dump for are enrolled Indians. This means that the Tribal cops and courts have no jurisdiction over the non-enrolled citizens, so now you have the County Sheriff or State Patrol, who have no jurisdiction over the Indians. It gets more convoluted when the victim is an Indian, or the perpetrator is non-Indian committing a crime to an Indian.

Stan just shakes his head at this chaos. But as he observes and reflects, he has discovered that this unorganized mess isn't really any worse than the circumstances off the reservation. In fact, in its own way, it's more honest.

G: Geriatric's. This book started with the statement that the guy that runs the Indian dump is not named Stan. His real name is not important. At first he corrected all the Indian customers at the dump when they referred to him as Stan. Many that came back the following week called him Stan again. As Stan reflected on it, he came to accept that it did not matter, and went with the new name.

So how did the Indians come up with "Stan"? Because it rhymes with man, as in "Stan the garbage man"? This Indian tribe has a cultural tradition of respecting and assisting "Elders". This tribe defines an Elder as any tribal man or woman that is fifty five years old, or older. Stan has no idea where that age originated. It certainly wasn't tied to Social Security retirement age. Stan reflected on the age, and history. Many moons ago, the average person died before they were sixty years old. The Indians had high incidents of diabetes. They had poor or no health care originally.

So Stan reflected that this age had simply been carried forward as a time honored tradition. Stan reflected that fifty five made a lot of sense. That's about when everything started to go south for him; his eyesight, hearing, sexual performance. STAN SAYS: "that was the second thing to go" when someone commented on his poor hearing or vision.

Stan crunches a lot of data mentally in his reflections. He has reflected that the Indian tribe is a microcosm culture indicative of the main stream population. Stan sees it in the trash. People don't like to hear it, but they buy their trash. The garbage company doesn't deliver it. It's not that they wouldn't, it's just that nobody has ever asked them to. STAN SAYS: "there's only three ways you get your trash; you grow it in your yard or garden, you buy it, or you allow someone to give it to you, like an inheritance".

Stan's dump accepts Elders free of charge as a matter of respect. The largest demographic in the United States is people turning sixty five. Of course Stan reflects, and crunches the data. First off, most of his customers are Elders. This is a duh because the Elders are free, of course you get mostly Elders. STAN SAYS: "free is the F word.

There is no free. The services that are not charged are subsidized by somebody else". But if you look at the big long term picture, this demographic is driving cell phone design and services, key board and software design, auto industry, health care, just about every aspect in human life, and in twenty years they will be gone, and things will change. STAN SAYS: "What does an Elder sing on the way out here? 'To the dump, to the dump, to the dump, dump, dump'" to the musical score of The Lone Ranger television show.

Stan has noticed that most of his customers, which are mostly Elders, are very active on Face book. The Indians even have their own Face book in which you have to be enrolled to log on. If Stan says anything to anyone, even a joke, he's dealing with it with every customer that follows. Stan has a lot of time. He has reflected that Mrs. Tule, who is around eighty years old, blind and deaf, mistook him for "Stan", when she asked his name, and because she had commented on his new bib overalls that day, and every customer that followed commented on Santa bringing "Stan" new overalls.

Why would anyone care? Naturally, Stan reflected. He reckoned that these Elders were lonely. Their kids were raised and on their own. They may not be employed full time. They've never done yard work, and can't recreate like they used to due to arthritis or bad joints. This Face book interaction allows them to be a part of a community of their peers that share many of the same issues, so Stan's new overalls are a big deal. "Yup, Stan got new overalls for Christmas". Stan agrees with Elsie Finley "Garbage never takes a day off". Her radiator in her old Ford pick-up leaks, so Stan saves antifreeze that comes in, and fills it when she comes. Of course everyone on Face book knows.

It forced Stan to adopt an overall policy. He began wearing farmer bib overalls about the time he turned fifty five. He got to where he had too much junk to carry in his regular pockets on his jeans; two cell phones, his wallet, which had a bunch of junk he hadn't looked at in three years, and was fat, three wads of keys, a couple note pads because he'd become forgetful, maybe a thumb drive or two, a knife, and some change.

The bib overalls have shoulder straps, just like a backpack, so it helped hold all this weight up. As he was gaining a little weight, his Wranglers no longer fit his waist anyway, and all these necessities would pull his pants down. Stan did have some style scruples. He was damned if he was going to wear suspenders. STAN SAYS: "you can't trust a man that doesn't trust his pants." Referring to men that wore both a belt and suspenders.

A component of Stan's bib overall policy was the timing. He wanted new overalls in the winter because they were heavier, and warmer. He preferred them worn in the summer when he worked in the heat. Then there's the color. Stan has multiple colors of overalls; as many as Cardhartt offers. He used to just buy the light tans and had several pairs of those. But folks thought that he never washed or changed his clothes because Stan was always dirty at the dump. So black one day, purple the next, green, tan, brown, light and dark, got cycled through. Of course it was all over the Elders Face book; what color Stan's overalls were today.

H: Transportation. Stan has come to recognize, through much reflection, that transportation is a quality of life issue, and even defines most people. Stan has traveled the United States, and foreign countries extensively. He has witnessed everything in regards to transportation. Stan himself has a one hour commute each day to his job at the dump on the reservation, and home again. He has reflected that he actually enjoys it. There is a cost, but he drives an old beater Nissan pick-up that was his wife's car, her first brand new car in her life, and she handed it down to Stan when she got her second brand new Nissan pick-up.

Stan see's wildlife every day. That is important to Stan. That's why he lives where he does; they have abundant wildlife on his farm. That's why his cats love his barn so much; some of this wildlife are predators; Coyotes,

Raccoons, Owls. They have a "kitty" door to a heated room for their safety.

But it is common for Stan to see coyotes, bald eagles, wild horses, bison, even bears, on his twice daily commute. He has been places like New York City, or London, where nobody in the entire history of the family has ever owned a car. They have always used public transportation, or rode a bicycle, or walked. Indeed the job location had determined where they worked.

Some of these folks became good friends that Stan stayed with, or vacationed with. It was interesting to Stan. As an example, Stan has always owned a car and driven it to work. Of course there are expenses beyond the vehicle cost; fuel, tires, maintenance (which Stan could perform himself), insurance. In New York just parking your car was prohibitively expensive, so most just took a bus, cab, subway, walked, bicycled, or a combination of all five.

Reflect on grocery shopping. New York doesn't have large super markets downtown. So first, you have to park. Then you need to go to the bakery, the butcher, the produce shop, maybe a staple supply house for toilet paper or paper towels, and then you lug all of your crap home, maybe in the rain or snow. What a hassle. That is one of the reasons eating out is so popular.

Stan knew several New Yorkers or Londoners that had a driver's license, they just didn't want to deal with the hassle of owning a car. So they used private or public transportation. They actually saved the money a car would cost for vacations, so they could ski in Aspen, or scuba in Grand Cayman for what owning a car would cost. Indeed, many of these vacations included renting a car, and they enjoyed their driving time, literally in the Outback, in Australia. Other friends of Stan's commuted in helicopters or airplanes. Stan was a fixed wing pilot at one time, and owned a thirty three percent interest in a Cessna 172. He sold his share when he realized that he did not fly enough to have instinctive reflexes.

So Stan's experiences of transportation are all over the board. He enjoys his long commute. He enjoys his Indian Elders. This commute allows him two hours of stress free reflection time with pleasant scenery, and no traffic. A lot of what Stan drives through is farm land; fruit orchards, hops, dairy cows. Most of this labor is Hispanic. The Americans refer to them as "Mexicans" but Stan has come to find that the "Mexicans" are above transient temporary farm labor, and work full time at a "real" job. Most of this Ag labor is from further south; many Guatemalans, even Hondurans and Uruguayans.

Stan dreads coming up on a line of cars going to work a field. This happens about once per week. First off, most of these drivers are kids, around eighteen years old. They have never driven a car; have no license, no insurance. The car was a "people mover" they bought pooling their few hundred bucks to purchase. They don't even transfer the title. They just drive it 'til it quits, and walk away.

Stan reflects that somehow, they find out about work

at a given farm, who knows how. This reservation is 1.4 million acres, so there are a lot of miles of farms. The packs of cars tend to run about seven to ten vehicles, with at least four people in each car. They drive along about five to ten miles an hour, one twenty feet behind the next, Stan reckons because only the lead car has someone that knows the farm. The line is too long to pass safely, and they're too close together to pass one at a time. Heaven forbid a school bus happens to get caught up in the pack. So Stan pretty much knows which crops come off when, or thinning or pruning season, and he has alternate routes. Stan reflects that Americans are so spoiled. If they had to pay the real cost for produce grown with legal Ag labor, they would scream bloody murder. Of course none of them would do the work themselves, it's too damn hard.

Stan reflects. These folks are mostly kids, most under twenty years old. They're about an even split, male to female. He has come to recognize that originally they sent money home to support relatives. But over time he has seen the cars morph into BMW's and Mercedes sedans, much nicer than his Nissan. He figures one of the reasons that they drive so slow in these modern high end cars is to save fuel. It's the same with their headlights. They'll putt along at dawn or dusk with no lights. Stan reflects that in their mindset, using your lights costs money, just like the electric bill in a house. He laughs when he sees "taco" trucks, or mobile food vendors at the site amongst the ten cars parked next to an orchard a few hours later, obviously there is some sort of organized communication. These "kids" are no longer sending money "home" and are "living the dream".

Stan has driven quite a lot along the Pacific Ocean in Mexico, from Mexicali to Mazatlán, and around Guadalajara. These roads are windy, with twists and turns going over hilly country. You can't see far ahead. It is common to see a driver drinking beer and throwing their empty bottle or can out the driver's window. What does it mean when you come up behind someone that has their left turn signal on? Not in central Mexico. They use their turn signals to let you know its okay to pass! So Stan does some serious reflection in the rear view mirror before he turns left.

To conclude this Transportation segment, Stan would ask you to reflect on his world; the garbage man goes down the right side of the street, stopping at every house, and collecting the garbage. Stan has learned that the route goes a lot faster if you go downhill as you load the truck, because the acceleration of the vehicle is faster, it's quieter, and uses less fuel. STAN SAYS: "make your living on the right road shoulder, you'll find that it's different out here". Once Stan was collecting trash on Terrace Heights Drive, which is a busy four lane arterial entering a city of 100,000 people. Stan was on the far right with all of his flashers, school bus stop lights, beacon, and work lights on. You could see his truck from outer space. He was actually right next to the garbage company shop and office.

It was just before eight o'clock, and winter, so it was just daybreak. Stan always watches the traffic behind him. He has known men that have been crushed between the back of a truck and a car. Stan saw a car approaching in the right lane as he dumped a can. He turned and faced the car. It was going about ten miles over the speed limit, forty five miles per hour or so. Stan reflected that's easy here because it's a good downhill grade. The person is probably coasting. As they got closer Stan could see a woman clearly leaned over to the rear view mirror applying her lipstick. Stan threw the can to the right off the road and began yelling and waving his arms like a deckhand on an aircraft carrier signaling a landing plane. She never looked away from her mirror. Stan jumped into the back of the truck, in the garbage, and from two feet away watched her airbag explode as she ran into his truck. The impact was so hard that it slid his truck ahead about two feet. Stan climbed out over her crumpled hood to check on her. She was conscious, but hurt bad, and her left eye was closed.

Stan went to his cab and used the two way radio to call the office, which was just over there, and requested an ambulance. He took his jacket over to cover her, but left her in the car for the paramedics to remove. In five minutes there were two police cars, two ambulances, and a fire truck. The woman had a red streak across her face from her mouth to her left eye. Stan see's this daily; men shaving, hair styling, make-up applications, brushing and even flossing teeth. Stan went to visit "Sarah" in the hospital. She was very apologetic. Stan felt bad even though there was nothing he could do. The only reason she hadn't lost her left eye was because she had the lipstick fully extended, and the cosmetic is soft, and her fist contacting her cheek stopped the forward thrust. Stan asked if she needed anything. Sarah thanked him and said no. Stan told Sarah that the truck, and the trash, was fine. She smiled with her one raccoon black eye. STAN SAYS "No brains, no headaches."

I. Politics'. Stan recognizes that this is a slippery slope. Stan will not attempt to tell you what to do. He may suggest what not to do,

based on his life's experiences, but he leaves the decisions to you. Stan has identified himself as a conservative Republican on political survey forms. He reckons it's mostly environmental. He lives in a rural farm area, sparsely populated. Stan knows that he does not like socialism. He's seen it firsthand in Argentina and the United Kingdom. He prefers capitalism, in that it creates employment and funds things (taxes). He has never really experienced communism, beyond Archie Bunkers narratives, but he reckons it is close to socialism, with a heavy handed government. The current Republican president is unpopular with the media, and gets a lot of criticism.

In Stan's lifetime he has had several presidents, from Lynden Johnson to Barrack Obama. There was Nixon, Clinton, the Bush's, Carter, Ford, and Reagan. Stan has reflected all this, and reckons that it just doesn't matter who the president is. Stan has heard the phrase "too big to fail" used to describe businesses. Stan reflects that maybe the founding fathers recognized the dangers of too much leadership power in too few hands, so we have the constitution, the three branches of government, and the states. By the time Stan has voted in his state the election is already decided, so it literally does not matter who Stan votes for.

Stan pays no attention to the mainstream media. He has experienced the media "spin" first hand, and has witnessed the advertiser power for media space. In one local election Stan had to get a large auto dealers permission to use some of his ad space in the newspaper. Stan only held an elected position once. He was a board member for a local fire district. Stan was not elected. There was a commissioner that moved to Arizona with three years left on his term. Stan was appointed by the other two commissioners and a city council. This was enough for Stan to know that it was not for him. An example was the local firemen wanted to take a fire truck three thousand miles to participate in a funeral parade for fallen firefighters from the 911 terrorist attack in New

York City. Stan was the deciding vote. He could not believe that they had the nerve to ask, much less expected to be allowed to go with the commissioners blessing. What about the lack of our truck and crew if we have an emergency? What about the cost, and the other demands that you have? Yes it's a tragedy, but what good would our truck and crew serve? Stan voted no. He is still hated to this day.

Stan reflects on the Indian politics. It is different, mostly nepotism combined with cronyism. Stan just chuckles. They do have elections, and "Council" meetings. They do pass laws, which generally are ineffective because there is little or no enforcement, and because the Indians are only about one quarter of the population of their reservation. He has worked with several, and considers them honest and well-intended, but since they have no taxing authority, and can't leverage their property for revenue to invest, they are just stuck in poverty.

An example is that they have outlawed alcohol on their reservation due to the detrimental effects to their members. There is no enforcement. Indeed you can drive to a grocery store or minimart and buy booze. The Tribe just trusts that people will comply. Stan reflects that this shows their true compassion to others. It also ties to their treaty. The treaty specifically states that allowing "spirits" on the reservation voids the treaty. In that symbolic way Stan reflects that the tribal leaders are dealing with the issues in their own way, even though to the average non-Indian it's just a big joke. The state that their reservation is in has legalized marijuana for recreational use. The tribe has not legalized its use, nor has the federal government. There is a lot of marijuana grown on the reservation, mostly within crop fields tended by the Hispanic Ag labor.

So generally Stan doesn't have much use for politicians. Stan reflects that the real work gets done by the little people. The politicians take credit for the success, but it's the garbage man that collects the trash, it's the CSR that answers the phone, and takes the heat.

Stan reflects that there are sincere folks that mean well when they enter the political game, but he has witnessed them turn their colors, and turn the position into their retirement program at other's expense. Stan is a big proponent of term limits. Not just elected office, but all public offices. Using the military as an example, the leader of a military installation can only be the commander there for a few years, except in a time of war. Stan has seen positive results from a fresh set of eyes every so often.

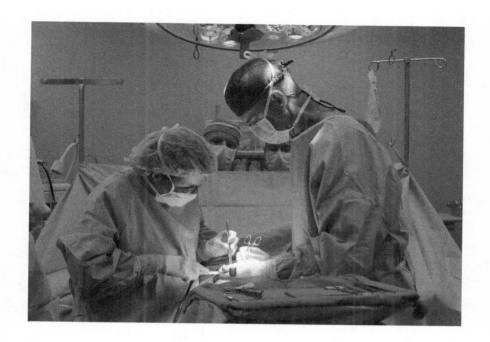

J. Healthcare. Well, Stan does have some personal experience with healthcare. Here Stan will tell you what not to do. STAN SAYS: "Don't do what I do". Stan has never had regular healthcare, other than a medical examination, what most call a physical, every other year to maintain his commercial driver's license. He has probably used a veterinarian and animal medications for his ailments more often than an MD.

Stan has broken multiple bones and had a lot of stitches, with no visit to an MD. He did go to a doctor, nine of them actually, when he broke his brain. He has gone decades with no personal physician. His distaste for the status quo medical world comes from two sources, both insurance related. First was the state Labor and Industries program for workers. Garbage men tend to be young, physically active, and if they require medical attention it is usually related to a workplace injury. Stan has protested a lot of L & I claims in his career due to no accident, false claims. This gets in to physicians statements, independent medical evaluations, and on and on.

One time Stan made an appointment with a physician to look at his neck pain. When his appointment finally arrived three months later, this doctor asked him to remove his polo shirt and describe his neck pain. Stan told her that he didn't need to remove his shirt, that she was the source of his neck pain. "Judy" as she came to be known later, was taken aback. Stan explained that she was treating one of his employees and she would not return his communications via, phone, US Mail, or email, that she was providing "palliative" care, which L&I won't pay for, and he wanted to know how to proceed with her patient, who was also his co-worker and friend.

Judy and Stan became friends over time. In fact, that is where Stan met his wife. Stan's accusation of palliative care was that L&I was paying for Viagra for back pain. Stan was no physician, but he had managed a lot of back pain claims that did not include Viagra. Dr. Judy schooled Stan that all patients have a legal right to "consortium" and that was why she prescribed the Viagra. This relationship went forward to include classes to the business community on how to manage L&I claims from a physician's point of view, which literally is the patients care and well-being.

Stan's other insurance related medical experience was when he broke his brain. He ended up with nine neurologists. His national insurance company assigned what they termed a "patients advocate". This woman had been a trauma nurse in her employment history. Stan's claim was nearing one million dollars with no improvement. As she interviewed Stan, he told her to be careful; that his brain was broken, and not only could he not process thoughts, he couldn't even "hold it" long enough to get to the potty. But her questions triggered his thought processes. What were these nine guys doing? All the nine doctors would say is "every brain is different, every injury is different, there's no 'standard' treatment for brain injuries, they're all different", and "how ya feelin?". Really? These frauds were milking the claim, and literally, not doing anything. Stan was home in a week, and his recovery improved significantly once he was out of the lockdown ward, and around all of his animals. All these nine neurologists were doing was LOJ, learning on the job, just like a garbage man learns a route.

Stan's wife is an RN. This frustrates her because he won't go to the doctor for a broken scapula, clavicle, ankle, stitches. STAN SAYS: "everyone I know that died went to a doctor".

Stan does have some positive medical experiences. Immediately after his daughter was born, like the next day, Stan took his wife at that time to the ER. She also was an RN. Stan held the baby while he waited in the waiting room. Dr. Sims, a pediatrician that was not their doctor walked by, nodded his head and kept going. About ten steps later he stopped, walked backwards the ten steps, and said "let me see that baby". He admitted her to the ICU in an oxygen tent where she spent the next week while her lungs developed. Stan's wife was a little disappointed with him when she came out of the exam room to no baby. STAN SAYS: "it's not as nice at the hospital when you don't have a room".

Stan would describe his health as "good", that he "gets up in the morning and nothing hurts, so it's a good day". But Stan does realize that one day, any day, he could die from a cancer, just like Dr. Judy did.

K. Weather. STAN SAYS: "if I could control the weather, I wouldn't take other people's garbage for a living". But Stan is very tuned in to his local weather. The dump he runs for the Indians is an "arid design" which means that it operates in a climate of less than seven inches of annual precipitation, including snowfall.

Stan is not a scientist. This "arid design" is not a product of his brain. The common worry with landfilling is ground water contamination from leachate entering the aquifer. The second worry is material's being landfilled that can be repurposed (recycled).

STAN SAYS: "there's two good things about garbage; everybody has it" and "nobody wants it". Keep in mind that Stan's opinion is that you buy your garbage. If you are a zealot, denying landfilling STAN SAYS: "don't buy it" and "good luck with that".

So the garbage trucks come into Stan's dump, and dump. They spread the loads out very thin, no more than two feet deep, at a shallow angle. The sun and the wind then evaporates any H2O into the atmosphere. If the loads were thick, this moisture would drain into the ground, developing "leachate". Stan once worked on a pyrolysis system with a Greek scientist named Strovos Mahail that his first "owner" hired. They developed a pyrolysis system. Stan was the fabricator. They got it to work, but not on an industrial scale. This machine was about the size of a semi, and it took a month to process one bag of trash from a residence.

But it left a lasting impression on Stan. Basically, ninety percent of all matter is moisture; your body, your car, your house, your trash. This moisture is what holds everything (your body) together. If you remove all of the moisture, what you are left with is about ten percent of the original volume that now looks like a cigarette ash. But pyrolysis is not burning. It is a scientific method that utilizes nature to remove the moisture, just like Stan's arid landfill.

Strovos culture interested Stan. He loved the Greek food with all the cinnamon. Strovos had family come over from the homeland, and he invited Stan to his home several times for dinner. Of course Stan did not understand any of the words, but they argued a lot, screaming at each other in Greek and waving their arms. Stan knew that Greece was on the Mediterranean around Turkey and Italy, but beyond that he was clueless. Stan felt odd being around these family fights. He asked Strovos if he should attend the dinners. Strovos responded "oh sure, there is nothing to worry about. As long as we are screaming everyone is still in love. It's when we get quiet that you have to worry".

Stan has gone around the block with recycling. He see's lots of stuff every day, nearly one half of all trash, that can be reclaimed, but there is a cost. Americans want it cheap, and they want it quick, and it better be good, Godammit! Stan is always amazed at how much food is thrown away. Stan and his wife won't throw food away. On many evenings their dinner is "Must Go", or leftovers. There are so many hungry people in the United States and around the world, that it is criminal to throw food out, in Stan's mind.

Stan's recycling dilemma is HDPE, high density poly eurathane, or a plastic milk jug. Of course it is "recyclable". First off, whatever happened to the milk man and the reusable glass bottle? Some new law that washed bottles weren't clean enough. So HDPE was originally designed from crude oil, as was most plastic. The oil industry has a huge lobby, and is politically connected, hence, laws. But America "needed" to get off of foreign oil, so what should we do? Along comes another huge lobby, the farmers. They started developing vegetable oil to run your tractors hydraulic system, make plastics, and on and on. More laws. Eventually our president got in a pissin' match with China, who was the only one taking our HDPE. Imagine the Chinese recycler. The crude oil HDPE won't blend with the corn oil HDPE, so he fired us, with this simple question; "why would you use your food to make your trash?"

Stan recognizes that someday in the not too distant future, for the United States to have an effective recycling infrastructure, we will have to move beyond the huge oil and farm lobbies. But a lot of America's needs can be made from recycled materials; cars, appliances, toys, furniture, packaging.

Stan has reflected. All of these dumps over time are repositories that can be mined at a later date. Stan has dug up a dump, looking for a dead body with the FBI. He was amazed how new a newspaper looked that was buried three years ago, like it was yesterday's paper. The FBI used the dates on the papers to narrow the dig down to their search date. Stan won't eat corndogs or Twinkies anymore. On one dig the FBI found a new jet boat on the trailer. That was a surprise. The Cat operator went to jail for insurance fraud, STAN SAYS: "just when you think you've seen it all".

Stan's other weather interest is his farm. He has forty acres, mostly in hay. It's a loser, but Stan needs to feed his critters. His banker calls Stan's neighborhood "white poverty" because the farming doesn't pay for itself. Stan works full time to support his farm.

So the weather is a reflection moment for Stan. He considers the fishermen in the Bearing Strait, or the Sherpa's climbing Mount Everest. Again, Americans are so spoiled. Sure there are a few hurricanes and the occasional volcano, but generally, if you're in the United States, you're pretty safe.

Stan can't stand cockroaches. There are none in his home region because of hard freezes every winter for three or four months. Stan has hauled garbage in the south. Cockroaches are common from Houston to Tallahassee. Indeed, many communities require twice a week garbage service, and the containers to be washed out when emptied. This gives Stan the shivers, and makes him appreciate his winters back home.

L: Pets. Stan has always had pets in his life, from an early childhood, except for a seven year stint after his first marriage when he spent most of his time traveling the world in jetliners. Presently, Stan has twenty critters that he feeds twice a day; eight polo ponies, six laying hens, four barn cats, two dogs. He also feeds out a couple steers and some hogs to slaughter and butcher for food. He grows his own alfalfa hay and barley.

Stan has reflected that animals come naturally to him, more so than people. Indeed, that is one reason that Stan's wife agreed to date a garbage man in the first place. She had three weenie dogs, which Stan thought crazy. Stan had always had a dachshund. When he tapped on her door on the first date he heard "RRRrrr, RRRrrr, RRRrrr, and RRRrrr!" He recognized their call immediately. She showed him in and he sat on the couch. One of her weenie dogs was a miniature murl named Shay-bunny. This mutt was stand-offish to everybody. As soon as Stan sat, Shay jumped up in his lap and started snuggling. Stan's wife to be figured Stan can't be that bad.

Some folks refer to it as "unconditional love". Stan does not believe in unconditional love. He has found that there are always conditions. STAN SAYS: "stop feeding them and see if they stick around".

Stan's wife is allergic to cats. Stan probably is too, but he reflects that his lifelong pursuit of trash has built up a natural resistance in his body to almost everything. STAN SAYS: "I haven't been able to smell since I was eighteen". One of Stan's four "barn cats" is a scraggly ass long haired black female named Foobie. She was dumped on Stan by his wife's daughters with some lame excuse. But again, this cat just took to Stan, like a faithful hound dog. Stan never really was a cat person, but you wouldn't know it watching him and Foobie.

Stan reflects that the problem with pets is that they depreciate so much faster than people. Stan had to euthanize his first horse at forty three years old! She had already had two previous owners, and killed them, so Stan reflects that he is the one that got away. But you don't have a good dog twenty years, so that means at sixty, you've gone through a lot of good hound dogs. Stan has had them for hunting, guard dogs, but mostly just lap hounds. The irony is that his wife used to show cats when she was an adolescent. Ever been to a cat show? Neither has Stan.

Stan love's his pets, probably more than all other people except his family. Stan wouldn't call it unconditional. None of them can bite him, and the horses can't kick him. Beyond that Stan has no conditions.

M: Holidays. Everybody loves holidays, right? Stan is no exception. The Indians have about fourteen paid holidays a year. At first Stan could not believe it! He had never experienced this level of generosity in the garbage collection business. Everybody just wants their garbage dumped on garbage day godammit! They got their holiday, but they could care less about the garbage man. "I pay my bill, I want my garbage dumped".

In fact Stan dreaded holidays in the garbage business. His company only took six; Christmas, New Years, Memorial Day, Fourth of July, and Labor Day, and Thanksgiving. As Stan's routing efficiency was maxed out per vehicle there was no "wiggle room" to pull two route days in one day, as most inefficient cities do. So

Thanksgiving is on Thursday. Everybody is off, the dump is closed. You have to do Thursday's routes on Friday, and then Friday's routes on Saturday. The days that the collection is one day late means that there is one seventh more volume in each can. One seventh doesn't sound like much until you extrapolate that across one hundred thousand cans, then it's an additional fifteen thousand cans!

So Stan would rather work Thanksgiving and have a normal weekend. Stan had worked in Canada some. Of course their holidays are different. There is no Fourth of July celebration, or Thanksgiving. But Canada is relatively Socialist in Stan's eyes, as opposed to the United States. Canada came up with a BC (British Columbia) Day just so that each month would have a three day weekend.

Stan's Indians are ahead of this game. Upon reflection, why would the Indians celebrate Thanksgiving? They don't celebrate Columbus Day. Oh they take the same holiday, but they call it "Indigenous Peoples Day" or "Native American Day" or some such fantasy.

Remember Elsie Finley's "garbage doesn't take a day off"? Stan thinks she's right. The garbage has to go. But the Indians want their fourteen holidays "just like everybody else". STAN SAYS: "everybody says that they want a full time job, 'til they have one".

N: Vacations. Vacations follow Holidays because, well the British call a vacation a "holiday". It could also fall under finances or relationships. Indeed Stan reflects that all of his categories encompass one effort; Life.

Stan's wife doesn't do well in the winter time. The grey skies, short daylight, cold, and being bound indoors do not suit her. She has tried tanning, and hot yoga, and snow shoeing, which help a little on a temporary basis, but Stan knows that he needs to get her somewhere warm and sunny during the months of December or January.

Stan has traveled a lot, at one time in his life nearly seven years non-stop, internationally, so he's had his fill of jets, airports, and customs. That is not to say that he does not enjoy travel, he does, mostly for the interaction with different cultures. Stan's wife takes to that also. On one trip to Argentina she was so enthralled that she seriously considered moving there for a year and working as a nurse.

Their vacations tend to pivot around financial windfalls, such as bonuses or tax returns. They don't save for them, probably because they are not that organized. Plus, when you have two dozen pets, ten of them scaling in at over one thousand pounds, it takes someone that knows what they're doing to babysit them. They don't want to impose on friends and family, plus their home is private, and, well, theirs. They both very much enjoy their home, and animals. But the winters are cold, dark, and four months long.

Stan and his wife have been to southern California in the winter, northern and west-central Mexico, Argentina, and Las Vegas. Usually they fly, but they have driven fifteen hundred miles. Some of these junkets were included in their employments. They are both high performers, on a salary, so bonuses at the end of the year are common for them.

Of course Stan reflects on vacations, and the Indians. The Indians have their own travel agency and credit union. They can get, say a trip to Disneyland, with little or no money down, and have monthly payments withheld from their paychecks. As stated earlier, the Indians can blow through money like Grant took Richmond, with no regard to any consequences down the road.

Stan has researched, and reflected. This Indian tribes lands were vast before 1850, nearly all of central

Washington State today, some fourteen to fifteen million acres. Prior to the white man, there were no horses. Travel was by foot, or canoe. They used dogs to pull drag along bundles on poles, and the Indians pulled them themselves. This "tribe" was actually fourteen regional bands and tribes thrown together by the U.S. military during the treaty process. So some of the bands or tribes never made it to another bands area in their lifetime. It is calculated that the "average" Indian never migrated more than fifteen miles in their lifetime prior to the horse. This small migration was chasing food; fishing in season, roots and grubs in season, and deer and elk. Of course their lifespans were short. The older Indians could not survive the harsh conditions.

This amuses Stan, and naturally, he reflects. The Indians never had a currency, and now they have a credit union? They never traveled more than fifteen miles, by foot, and now they haul their trash to their dump in a Cadillac Escalade and take their kids to Disneyland? When he asks his Elder customers about it, they joke with him. It's okay to joke about the Indians as long as it's them doing the joking. Stan has learned via the Face book connections that he doesn't dare joke about it himself. Stan has witnessed this around other cultures in America. The black men would call each other "niggers", but Stan better not. STAN SAYS: "there are wise men, and there are otherwise".

Q: Career. Stan doesn't call taking other people's trash a career. Stan is amused by folks that "attempt to make a silk purse out of a sow's ear". He has heard terms like "Sanitation Engineers" and "Solid Waste Technicians" to describe his efforts to pay the bills, but he prefers "garbage man". Stan reflects that it is more honest, and descriptive. As Stan reflects, he considers other cultures. Most nations do not have professional sports. Their efforts stop at the Olympic level, and Stan considers some Olympic sports to not actually be sports. If they're going to hand out gold, silver, and bronze for curling and ice sweeping, why not billiards and bowling?

But Americans have made careers out of baseball, football, basketball, boxing, and a host of other endeavors. Stan has been around several professional athletes, and frankly, he pities them as people, totally clueless to reality, like other celebrities in film and politics'.

The Indians have some of their own sports and games. Stan is thrilled by these as they tend to be more down to earth, and honest. They have "wild horse racing", which is akin to American rodeo bronc riding before rodeo went corporate. They have "stick games" which is a form of gambling akin to craps. They have all sorts of drumming, dancing, and singing competitions. Stan reflects. One phenomenon across the United States is Indian casinos. Gambling is regulated in most states, and in Stan's experience, gambling formally is only allowed in Nevada and Atlantic City. But the Indians can have a casino on their reservation. Stan's tribe has a casino. Indeed all the Indian casinos compete with each other for gamblers. Of course the Indians don't have any money, unless a big check just came out, so the casino's host entertainment to draw visitors. As Stan reflects he has drawn a conclusion. The Indian casinos are "The Great Equalizer" in Stan's view.

Stan and his wife like to gamble, but they don't enjoy the Indian casinos. Stan considers them "clanging bells and stale cigarette smoke". Stan considers them "all the same" which is rare for Stan, to group a people together. These casinos try to create jobs for enrolled members. Stan likes roulette, but the payouts are complicated on multiple splits, which is what Stan likes to play. "It's no fun if you get a clod". Stan has never found an Indian roulette wheel operator that had a clue. Stan reflects that these Indian casino employees have a "career" which is more than he can say for himself.

"The Great Equalizer" means that generally, Indians are still looked down on by mainstream Americans. There are multiple reasons for this that varies by geography. But an Indian can enter an Indian casino and be treated just like everyone else; they can sit at a slot machine and have a free drink served by a waiter or waitress. They can smoke. Indeed the waitress may light their cigarette. They can be proud that this "is their casino".

Stan's career path is more what Stan calls a career trap. He did not go through formal training like the Indian roulette wheel operator. He did not choose this path like the high school science teacher. He was just there, at the right or wrong time, with some natural mechanical ability and a strong work ethic, and just never stopped. STAN SAYS: "don't stop moving, you'll seize up". Stan's wife is similar. Of course she went to college to get an RN's license, but she actually had to go back to college when she had moved too high in the organization for a nurse to hold her position. She still says; "I'm just a nurse". Actually, at the rare times that they are at a civic function, they both claim "to be chicken farmers" when they are introduced, because everyone wants "something free" from the garbage man or nurse. STAN SAYS: "free is the f word". Stan's wife doesn't want to spend the evening discussing someone's mother's incontinence. They actually are chicken farmers. They have six "Americana's" that lay two brown and four blue eggs every day.

So Stan and his wife both share humble beginnings, and just worked their asses off. Nothing was handed to them. They have a good lifestyle, but they earned it. They both consider themselves just plain common folks. STAN SAYS: "you know you're a redneck when you have five pick-up trucks, and no car". Stan and his wife have discussed this. He is a little older and will retire first. She has a lot of stress. He has offered to have her quit her job, and just stay home. She refuses. She wants her freedom, which her income allows. So career wise, Stan doesn't really know what he wants, and never has. He just knows what he doesn't want. STAN SAYS: "the good thing about garbage is everybody has it, and nobody wants it". Stan reflects that that is the perfect business model, and as close to guaranteed job security as you'll (he'll) ever find.

P. Sex. <u>To repeat;</u> Stan will not tell you what to do, or how to do it. Particularly with this subject matter. Stan's wife's first view of this is, well, right now, so wish her happiness, freedom, and contentment. Hi Honey! This is not about sexual orientation. Stan's has good friends and family on both sides of the aisle. STAN SAYS: "if you have to ask, who cares?" So again, Stan will only offer advice on what not to do, based on his life's experiences.

Stan's first suggestion is that you don't moan out the wrong name in the heat of passion. Stan has never committed this foopah, but he has received it, from his second wife just before she ran off with the electrician at the hospital. Stan can tell you that it is a certified boner buster. STAN SAYS: "you can have sex by yourself; it's just not as much fun".

Stan understands that his partner may need to fantasize about someone else to reach climax with him, after all, he's the Indians dump guy. He has had that naked talk to the mirror suggested in the beginning of this book. He can see the down side. But if you're fantasizing, or if you're with Stan, Honey, when you're fantasizing, use the inside voice, not the outside voice.

There's always a lot of trash talk around garbage men, not actually about trash, but about sex. Many like to brag about size, endurance, how good they are, how many times they get it, and on and on. Stan just reflects. STAN SAYS: "it's always been big enough to satisfy me"! Stan did get some advice that he has remembered from an Indian "when you feel like you can't hold it anymore, but you need to go a little longer for her sake, envision Lassie getting run over by a Greyhound bus." Stan has tried it. It works, too well.

So again, this could be under relationships or even finances for some folks, but there is no straight arrow. You just gotta be what you are, and find someone that is willing to accommodate that. Just reflect on what is important in your life, and be open and honest, and try to meet each other's needs, or desires. Stan has written off sex for periods of his life. Both of his ex-wives ran off with their co-workers. Stan gave up drinking at the same time. He just did not want to create any bigger problems for himself, his children, or his garbage company. STAN SAYS: 'that's the screwin' you get for the screwin' you got".

In this manner, about the only thing Stan can advise about sex, is what not to do. Some cultures are very open to the topic. Stan finds this interesting, because Americans are not open to discussing it, but it is an accepted form of entertainment. Stan has attempted Face book, in self-defense. To Stan it is just another form of porn. It would appear so by the selfie's from India and everywhere else that show the outstanding cleavage, but the face is cut off at the nose. I guess she has her priorities. Maybe so her mother, or husband, can't see her face. Stan doesn't bother. In one conversation Stan had with a seventy six year old Indian, he asked "how old do you have to be before you stop wanting sex?" The old Indian replied "you'll have to ask someone older than me".

Q: Sports. Stan is not a jock. However, sports have always been a part of Stan's life. His career as a garbage man is athletic, almost in a military training sort of way. The garbage man starts early. He works hard all day. His first employer had all of his routes set at around an eight hour casual day. If you hustled you could get it done in seven, or even six and a half hours. You still got paid for eight hours, but all missed stops, or accidents, came out of your pay. So many actually ran on their routes. You develop a sort of rhythm, and it's either hot, or cold, or windy. The down side is the dogs always chase a running garbage man, and several got run over chasing the truck. Those stories could be their own book, because once "Muttly" was dead he all of a sudden became some ultra-trained hi-bred worth a bazillion dollars. STAN SAYS: "why do you leave Muttly out if he's so valuable"?

So the garbage man is fit. He / she runs and lifts heavy bulky objects all day. He / she does not eat lunch, because, well, the trash does not enhance the palate. Several of Stan's co-workers were actually body builders that entered competitions. Many of these took hormones or steroids for muscle enhancement. There is a stress that fits a garbage man called "going postal". It is a reality Stan has experienced. The average person is hard working, and attempts to stay "caught up" or even tries to "work ahead" in their job. Garbage collection is extremely repetitive. Always the same truck, the same route every week, the same heavy can, the same biting dog, every week, it's always the same. Stan has seen some that require this repetition to maintain their calm. They can't handle a change of scenery or dealing with "surprises."

Of course there are sick days, vacation, or somebody quits or gets fired, and a "trainee" which could be a twenty year employee, has to "learn" your route. There is a kid on Stan's Tuesday route that he calls Dennis the Menace. This is at 5205 Pear Butte Drive. Stan has a warning printed every week, what they call "a running dispatch", to warn anyone "blind" on his route. They have two thirty two gallon galvanized cans next to a fence about ten feet from the house, or "a 100 foot pack-out" in the industry vernacular. Dennis always plays some nasty trick. Of course the driver is hustling. One time Dennis shoved a cat in the can and put the lid on, so the next morning when Stan pulled the lid off, "RRRRRRR" as the cat jumped out onto Stan's face clawing for traction. Another time Dennis placed an electric iron at the bottom of the can, and ran the cord up out the top and tied it to the fence. He then placed loose trash, out of the garbage bags, over the iron and concealed both it and the cord. Stan ran up to the can, grabbed it and left on the run for the truck, and the iron came to the end of its cord and pulled Stan to the ground spilling trash everywhere.

So between these challenges of practical jokers, heavy cans, traffic, and holiday schedules, your garbage man can be on edge. Add in the body builder taking steroids and you get what Stan calls "Roid Rage". They become extremely violent. Stan has seen garbage men chase vehicles with their truck and actually drive the truck through the entrance windows and doors into a grocery store chasing their customer that slighted them in some way. STAN SAYS: "it's not just the meth heads you need to keep an eye on."

Stan has always been involved in some sport, all of his life, although they may not be "conventional" sports. Sure he participated in cross country, basketball and baseball in high school, until he got his driver's license and started working full time after school. He never really excelled at any of these sports, partially because he was small, a year younger than everyone else, and he was scrawny, literally a ninety pound weakling. He had older brothers that were very good in sports, but he just did not have the drive. But he did either start, or was the first substitute in the game, so he wasn't the worst player on the team.

Stan's first unconventional sport outside of organized school play was drag racing. Stan joined the NHRA (National Hot Rod Association) and began drag racing in Gas, Modified Production with a fifty five Chevy that he built himself with a 427 big block L-88. He was making good money at sixteen, and living at home. He built the car after work (swing shift) in the shop that he worked in. He also turbocharged an XS 1100 Yamaha bike and drag raced that, He could do one hundred forty miles per hour in a quarter mile in about nine seconds. The front wheel was off the ground almost the entire quarter mile.

His next sport went a different way. Some would not call it a sport, more of a hobby. But there were self-help books to deal with stress, and physical and financial conditions, it required a lot of time, and there was physical activity, so in that way it was sport, to Stan. He competed in scale model radio controlled aircraft. He actually was pretty good, and had some regional success. When you fly a radio controlled airplane away from you, the controls are conventional for up, down, right, left. When the airplane turns one hundred eighty degrees, the up and down are the same, unless you're inverted, then their backwards, but the right and left are reversed, unless you're inverted. Stan built and tested these aircraft after work in the shop that he worked in. Some of them were large enough that you could place a cat inside, and they could kill you, if they hit you.

Stan fished, hunted, shot skeet, and trapped for furs. Stan took up polo at forty three years old. He had never ridden a horse. He enjoyed this immensely. Polo is not a big deal in the United States any longer. But it is in Mexico, Canada, Europe, and South America. Stan loved the animals, and the variety of cultures that he played with, along with each nation's polo history. World War One was the decline of polo. Most of the horses were lost in the war. In Stan's reflections and investigation, he found that his Indians had a huge impact on polo locally, before "the war".

Stan had a serious head injury in polo the day before his fifty third birthday. He sheared his brain and spent a month on life support in a coma with two ribs through his lungs. When he came out of the coma, in a lockdown mental ward, this is where Stan embraced mortality. The horse and the helmet were fine.

Stan reflects on his Indian customers sport mentality. Most of these folks are around sixty, and in poor shape. Diabetes is a common ailment with this group. But they have on really expensive pro football jerseys with the number twelve on the back for "the twelfth man", or black leather Superbowl jackets, both of which Stan cannot afford, nor would he buy them if he could. Is football some ancient Indian tradition? Doubtful in Stan's mind. He knows where several of these folks live, and drives past their place on occasion. They have taken a blue, or green, or both, can of spray paint and painted the number twelve on their roll-up garage door. Really?

Stan reflects. He reckons it's just like the Face book crowd. For twenty bucks they can buy a can of paint and a half case of beer, and sit and watch a game in which they are a part of a Superbowl team effort. They can go down to "their" casino, and bet on the game. They are not alone; they are an active part of something really big! Sport means something different to every individual, just like sex, and racism. It's environmental, social, a part of your living circumstances.

Stan reflects that polo used to be an international game that competed in the Olympics. Stan would like to see that return. As Stan understands the issue, the problem is the transport and quarantine of all the various animals from all over the world. The "fix" is to have a lot of horses in that country, and draw lots for the animals for each team. STAN SAYS: "the most expensive horse I ever owned was free", and "polo is like sex. You can do it by yourself, but it's not as much fun, and "the problem with polo is you get polo people, the horses are fine".

R: Philosophy. Stan reflects that he should cut and paste this to (P). or even 3(P). For Philosophy, Psychiatry, and Psychology. Of course all three words have a different definition, but to Stan, following his brain injury, they're all the same; a brain function. As Stan reflects it could also go under Sex because that is a mental effort as well as physical.

Stan is certainly not going to attempt to advice you on how to think. In fact Stan doesn't accuse many people of thinking, certainly not the reactionary folks. STAN SAYS: "take people at face value until they give you a reason not to". This has bit Stan in the butt a time or two, mostly over money and horses, but he still holds that value close to his heart. STAN SAYS: "there are wise people, and there are otherwise".

So the Buddhists Stan has talked to have a suggestion. "Choose what is close to your heart". Their philosophy is that Americans have too many desires. No matter how much they have, they want more. When your body expires your spirit lives on in others, but you can't take your treasures with you. Stan reflects that the Indians "Creator" teachings mirror the Buddhists in a strange sort of way. He wonders if that goes way back, like ice bridges to Asia many moons ago.

Stan has researched it, and reflected. There used to be several Japanese families on this reservation, which were Buddhists. After Pearl Harbor everyone of Japanese descent was rounded up and shipped inland a thousand miles to internment camps. They lost everything. Most did not return following the two atomic bombs Uncle Sam dropped on Japan.

So at Stan's hot yoga "practice" his Zen Master (Stan's term) advises "pare down your desires to one or two. Hold those close to your heart. You cannot obtain peace and contentment if you have too many desires". Stan has found that this philosophy from this sport really does work for him. Stan desires nothing for himself. He appreciates that he gets up in the morning and nothing hurts, too bad. He appreciates the weather, even when it's bad. He appreciates that his animals are fine. He appreciates his wife. He appreciates that he eats well, and has all the food anyone could ask for. Stan reflects that he would like to be younger again, but he appreciates that he has lived this long.

Stan would have you make a fist with each hand and then join them at your thumbs. That is about the size and shape of your brain. Now slide your hands apart an inch or so. That is what your brain looks like after you sheared it. There is a lot of science and medical studies around right and left hemispheres and brain lobes. Stan only knows what he experienced.

Consider your "non-directed" brain functions. Stan will use eyesight for his example. When you want to focus on something you squint your eyes. But when you look over your right shoulder to change lanes you don't direct your eyes to track each other and focus, they just do. Same thing when you look ahead again, your left eye tracks your right eye and you focus, automatically. Not so if your brain is sheared. There are no automatic functions. Your eyes don't track and focus automatically. You can't "hold it" 'til you get to the potty.

The RN's in the lockdown ward called Stan a "sharter". He did not understand and took offense. His RN told him that TBI (Traumatic Brain Injury) patients cannot fart and hold it at the same time, so "NO FARTING". She told Stan "if you have to fart, be sitting on a toilet". One of the nine neurologists Stan had explained it like this; "Imagine your commute to work or school. You have a route that you travel on that commute. All of a sudden there is an earthquake, and a giant canyon now crosses your path. You don't quit your job or school; you just take an alternate route. That is what your brain has to do, for the rest of your life".

It's literally like being an infant again; going potty, reading, writing, math, going up and down stairs, driving a car, using an ATM, riding a horse, everything. Stan learned that food is not what you think. He had never considered how important texture was to him. If it tasted good, Stan wolfed it down. Not so after the brain shear. You expect a nacho chip to be crunchy, and a spaghetti noodle to be gushy. What if they were reversed? Would that be good food? Stan's tongue, lips, and mouth could not discern texture, so Stan just stopped eating, and lost about fifty pounds. His wife had to make him choke down protein milkshakes to stay alive.

Stan came up with some weird quirks, like he just absolutely had to know what time it was, even if it didn't matter. He was constantly rolling over in bed, all night, every night, to see what time it was. Stan's wife researched a digital clock that reflects the time onto the ceiling so that she could get some sleep. It probably is no coincidence, but about the only thing consistent with the pre-brain shear Stan was his care for his animals. Stan reflects that there is something deeper than mental there.

There was some humor. Neurologist Number Eight took great delight in removing Stan's driver's license from his wallet, cutting it into little pieces, and exclaiming "you will never drive again". Scooby Doo's words came to mind, which all of a sudden, post brain shear, was more common; "rass role!" Stan's wife got him in several physical therapy and doctors assessments with her connections, which Stan owes his life to. He had to drive with a physical therapist named Marylou to gauge his brain / body functions. While they are driving down the freeway, Stan just pulls off to his right. Marylou screams and yells "what are you doing?" Stan points to the window with his index finger as the ambulance races past. Stan passed, and drives today, but his wife is still nervous. Neurologist Number five informed Stan that it takes on average about seven years for a TBI patient to resume "normal" life. Stan reckons that's a conservative number, in fact, that some things will never be the same, and that's probably good. Stan has had a lot of comments from garbage men like "you're a lot nicer to be around".

Of course Stan reflected. He discovered that some eighty percent of all TBI injuries are youths under sixteen in sporting accidents, or car wrecks. This saddens Stan; to be denied "normal" life before you've even experienced it. Stan reflects that he is lucky, and grateful, that his TBI was later in his life.

To sum up Stan's view on philosophy, he would suggest that you have that talk with that guy in the mirror. Be honest with yourself. Decide what is important to you, and what is not. There may be reasons, but they're your reasons. So just decide what is important to you, and be true to yourself. Accept what falls in line with your priorities, and reject what is not. For some it may be a certain religion, for others not so, or politics'. Surround yourself with folks that share your priorities. Don't judge others, just leave them be.

S: Food / budget. Again, Stan recognizes that this topic could be under finances, or even relationships. Stan has decided that food should go under Life for the obvious reason. Stan tagged budget to food because he reflects that Americans don't even consider the cost of food in their daily lives. They just buy whatever they want, even though they probably should not from a health perspective. STAN SAYS: "you are what you eat."

As mentioned throughout this book, Stan and his wife not only grow their own food, they grow the food that their food eats. It is amazing to Stan, how well the vegetable garden does on the chicken manure; much better than store bought fertilizers.

So Stan has been around the block. Most Americans

have an informal budget in their head. An Americans idea of a formal budget is a calendar with the house payment or rent, car payment, etc scribbled down on a payday. There's the utilities, TV, internet, cell phone, car insurance, maybe daycare. But there is never food. The average American does not spend ten percent of their income on food. Wardrobe and dry cleaning may be in the "budget" but not food.

Other cultures spend as much as ninety percent of their liquidity on food, or more. Stan and his wife appreciate their food, and realize that they are more fortunate than almost everyone else in the world, in this regard. Stan and his woman don't want to go out to dinner. They enjoy their food, and home, more than any restaurant. One thing they enjoy is giving away their food. They have more than they can eat. But friends and family really enjoy the eggs, bacon, hams, roasts, steaks, and other items that they receive. Stan's wife gives food as tips to her hairdressers, coworkers, and others. They enjoy it so much that they want to buy into the process. Of course it is a lot of work, every day. Cows don't take a day off. It is not cheap. They can buy meat cheaper than what theirs costs. But the taste is unbelievable, and all of your shopping is done, for a year. Stan has five freezers.

Food is very cultural, and they do study it and test various herbs and other flavors and cultures. Stan's wife has learned to make her own pizza and ravioli dough's from "pulish" and other recipes. Some of these cultures are basically molds that were grown, that they learned at wineries of all places.

Stan can't remember the last time he ate "fast food". Keep in mind that forty years ago all he ate was cheeseburgers from Rossow's-U-Tote 'em, every single day. Stan has worked in "servant" cultures wherein the servants prepare the meals for the patron's family, but they eat separately in a different building. A lot of these regions' had no power, or unreliable power, so meals were prepared the old fashioned way. Often there was no refrigeration or freezing. Most of them used "clay ovens" in that a sort of dome was built from clay above a clay base to help control the draft, and exit the smoke. A fire was made with wood, usually in the center, but sometimes to one side. You then cooked your meal next to the coals. Stan learned a lot from watching these meal preparations. Stan and his wife have an old wood cook stove that they prefer to use in the winter. It is too hot in the summer.

So Stan doesn't have his food budget under finances because no other American considers it either. To an American, food just is, like the air that you breathe. When an American goes grocery shopping, indeed, a good part of their purchases' is not food; toilet paper, paper towels, soaps, the pets' food, even entertainment devices.

As Stan reflects, he is glad that Americans are so spoiled. It certainly wasn't this way prior to World War Two. Stan regrets that any human being should be hungry. Stan is surprised how many people think that it is their inherent right to be American. STAN SAYS: "nobody can control who their parents were". But as Stan reflects all issues, any person could have been born into any circumstance around the world. A person's true character is what they do with those circumstances, whether it be race, gender, nationality, geography, religious beliefs, finances, or health.

I: Salvaging. So if you are thinking that this topic is about digging through others discards, you are wrong, sort of. There are all sorts of discards in life other than material items; People, pets, ideas, dreams. Stan has been around a lot of salvaging, indeed his entire adult life. Stan has been discarded himself more than once. Stan actually coaches all the new garbage men about salvaging. STAN SAYS: "You'll drag stuff home every day for your first year. You'll drag stuff back every day for the rest of your career". Stan really thinks he can claim that he has seen it all regarding salvaging. Indeed, it is a safety concern for Stan. People adopt a sort of salvaging panic over grabbing an item before the bulldozer pushes it up. Stan had a co-worker back when he was on nights in a big city; Benny. Benny's job was repairing garbage containers. There were thousands, and only so much shop space, so the container bay was triple shifted. Benny had grabbed an old container from out back and filled it with shoes. This was a system he had worked out with a driver. There were six hundred and forty left shoes. This particular store was a high end shop downtown that had a generous "no questions asked" policy on returns. They completely changed their stock from winter to spring.

Stan just happened to run across this while he was looking for a certain kind of dumpster. Benny had done this for years. When Stan was snooping around out back in the dumpsters, Benny demanded to know what he was doing. Stan told him "It's on a need to know basis" and simply walked away. But it did get Stan's curiosity up.

Benny's scam was that this high end department store threw away all of the left shoes first, with about half the boxes. In a month or so the six hundred and forty right shoes would arrive, with the other boxes. Benny and this driver would return the shoes in the boxes for a cash refund. They had all sorts of family and friends join in so it was not noticed as the same person returning all the shoes. They would keep whichever they liked, that fit, and even wore those into the store on the "return" trip.

Stan did not tell, but he did observe the loads from this store following Christmas, and the holiday shopping, and the following sales events were over. They must have figured it out, Stan reckons a computer reconciling the returns to the disposed models, but eventually the shoes had a cut from a razor knife a few years later.

So just like every other category, this one could fall under several other topics. All in all, it's life.

As mentioned earlier, Stan's Indian customers can blow through cash like nobody's business. Indeed, Stan see's several items thrown away, almost daily, that sometimes are still in the original packaging. Stan has a safety concern. He wants all children to stay inside the vehicle so that they don't get hurt, Stan's dump has a lot of rattlesnakes as well. An example is a small child's bike. When you are four or five years old you need a small bike. It doesn't take long to outgrow that bike, and it has to be replaced. Stan gets a lot of small bikes. He just lines them up along the fence and lets anyone take one that wants one. Often parts are robbed.

Of course there is Face book, and his inventory is all over that, with pictures. A lot of the Indians are yard sale enthusiasts. Stan is not. Stan hates yard sales, and refuses to have one. The Indians are all over the yard sale scene statewide, and even have preferential areas where "the stuff is better". STAN SAYS: "garage sales are just garbage sales without the b".

Stan has other salvaging concerns. This tribe has a serious infestation with bedbugs. It is rampant. When you treat a home for bedbugs, a lot gets thrown out; clothing, linens, beds, furnishings. Stan see's "good stuff" every day. He council's folks to stay away from the items.

Usually all he has to do is mention "the b word" and they all vamoose.

One time an Elder, Arlen, was there first thing in the morning, actually while Stan was unlocking the gate. Arlen is a regular and knows the drill, so Stan just lets him go on about his disposal business. Stan has a transfer station to keep the residents off of the working face of the landfill, for safety, one of which is salvaging. Nobody can resist cases of brand new potato chips or cereal boxes still in the original packaging. Mindful of the six hundred and forty pairs of shoes, Stan wants the business community to be assured that their disposal items are actually buried in the landfill. STAN SAYS: "if the ranch dip is past the expiration date, don't eat it!"

So Stan looks out his pay shack window a few hours later, and there is Arlen's pick-up parked next to the dumpster with no Arlen. Stan hears Scooby Doo's "Ruh Ro" in his head and goes out to investigate. Arlen is inside a forty yard drop box digging through the garbage. "Arlen, what the flip?" Arlen explains that he lost his cell phone, and reckons that it fell out of his chest pocket while he was throwing his trash out. "Can you call my cell and see if it rings?" which makes sense, except that Arlen followed that with "I don't see any of my own trash."

Stan explained to Arlen that this box was hauled and dumped a few hours ago, and his garbage is buried by now, in the landfill. This is fairly common. Couples get in arguments and throw their wedding ring away. After some time they reconsider, and want to find their ring. Now all of a sudden it has sentimental value. But Stan has gone through the loads out of a truck, and located their trash based on their description of what kind of bag they use, or what was thrown out with it, and actually recovered the ring. It is not uncommon.

So salvaging can be taken literally, such as digging something out of the trash, or rhetorically, such as saving a soul, marriage, or an animal's life. Stan reflects that he hopes that the crack addict infants that were rescued from a dumpster eventually found a good life and made a way in the world for themselves. Stan can't fathom what that must be like for whoever took on that challenge, but heah, good for them.

So there are as many forms of salvaging as there are things that need salvaged, whether that is a person on drugs, or alcohol, a feral cat, a slow racehorse, or an unattended pit bull.

For some this rescue is religion. For others it is family support. Stan reckons that the military is one form of salvage for many. There is structure and purpose, and plenty of space to move ahead, all things many may have never experienced in their life.

Stan would suggest that everyone should experience this at some point in their life. STAN SAYS: "saving one cat will not change the world, but saving one cat will change that cat's world, forever".

Stan has never witnessed a foster parent scenario that

he would call "positive". But as he reflects, he realizes that even though it is not necessarily good, at least it is better than where they were. Stan sees a lot of this with the Indians. He see's young children being raised by grandparents. Stan does not know the particulars. Maybe it's a work schedule situation, or some other problem. As most of the Indians are related in some way, there is family support, but again, Stan reflects that often that influence is negative.

Like most of life's issues, there is no silver bullet, no straight arrow. If each person would reflect, and consider if they could at least do something, one little thing outside themselves to help, the world would be a better place, and so would that person.

So whether it's the homeless, the dog pound, the old folks home, the school, or church, Stan asks that you reflect. You may have to lose some of your preconceived opinions. Not every homeless person wants a home. They are content right where they are. Do not force yourself on others. Do not judge them.

Stan served on a juvenile sentencing deferral board at one time that was titled "the Youth Accountability Board". His "client" was a nice young lady around thirteen years old named Ashley. She was an only child from an affluent family. Both of her parents were at the intervention, which was in the County Juvenile court complex. Both parents were smartly dressed with all the "accessories": A Rolex watch, the big rock wedding ring, which they flaunted above the meeting table. Ashley's dad was determined. He was going to "fix" this problem. Stan sat on one side of a table and had her file. She was between her parents on the other side of the table. Stan introduced himself, and Ashley's father introduced her, and nudged her to offer her hand. Stan did not shake her hand. He gently took her right hand in his, looked her in the eyes, and squeezed her fingers. Stan explained the deferral process; that she would have to serve eight hours of community service, the same time as a night in jail. She asked Stan what he did for work. He replied that he was a garbage man. Her mother actually laughed. The goal of this program was to allow people under eighteen years old that were first time offender's to do community service or some alternative to incarceration. Indeed the juvenile jail had a lot of gang members and drug dealers, so one goal of the program was to limit their exposure to "new friends".

There aren't that many jobs a juvenile can perform. What there is are things like picking up litter along the fence lines in the city parks or school yards. The kids hated any school assignments because everyone would see them. They were required to wear "prisoner uniforms" while they completed their task, which was simply orange coverall's with DOC on the back shoulders. Both of her parents were dressed very nice, as if going into court. Stan had his uniform on as he came straight from work. Stan reckons that the parents were expecting an attorney or judge. The girl's mother asked "what are you going to make her do, pick up garbage?" Stan answered "I wish I could. Child labor laws won't allow it."

Stan knew how this was going to go. He's seen it a million times. Her parents were clueless. As Stan thumbed through the file he asked her to retell her story of her shoplifting arrest. She explained that she was at the store with a baggy sweatshirt on. She grabbed the item, stuffed it under her sweatshirt when she thought nobody was looking, and took it to the restroom.

Stan reached across the table and took both of her hands in his. She was startled, and her mother shifted in her seat like she was going to intervene. Stan looked directly into her eyes and asked "was it positive or negative?" The girl burst out in tears. Stan continued looking into her eyes. The parents were bewildered. After several sobs she responded "positive" and folded her arms under her head. Technically, she had never left the store with the item, but she did use it before paying for it,

Stan reflected. There are bigger problems here, like your parents don't even know that what you stole was an early pregnancy test kit. He reflected on the infants that they found in dumpsters, and abortion. It was not Stan's place to intervene. He did not know if this family was religious, and if so what faith, or what her parents did for a living.

Stan asked her what she thought she could do for the intervention job. She did not know. He offered painting over graffiti with him, after school. Her "sentence" would be eight hours of community service. Her mother objected "I don't want my baby around other people's trash!" Stan asked her opinion. "What about picking up litter like the other kids get?" Stan said "well we can do that, but it's still picking up other people's trash". Stan asked the girl what she thought. She said that she would rather paint over the graffiti.

Stan completed the diversion form and they agreed to a schedule; four hours beginning tomorrow afternoon. Stan didn't know what he was going to do. He was just going to let this little pregnant girl know that somebody gave a shit, and probably relay his infant in the dumpster stories. It would probably be a good experience for her to meet some of the girl gang members and talk to them about their lives. Ashley certainly did not get that experience at home. Stan never found out how things worked out. Following her two days of graffiti removal Stan never saw or heard from her again. He reflected that the girl, and the baby, were "salvaged" by someone. He wished he could do more, but Stan's just a garbage man. Stan reflected that Ashely's clueless parents get something out of it, and become more involved in her life.

U: Charity. This subject is a bit like salvaging, in Stan's eyes. There are all types of charity, from the receiving angle, to the giving side. In regards to the former, Stan has had friends on welfare or food stamps. They were so embarrassed that they did their grocery shopping at midnight so nobody that they knew would see them. This breaks Stan's heart. On the opposite side of the same coin he has stood in line behind folks that have "accepted" items, and paid with food stamps, then a separate pile of "unaccepted" stuff Stan can't afford, and watches while they peel a hundred dollar bill off a roll of cash. This also breaks Stan's heart.

Stan does not claim to have the answers to all the

world's ills. Archie Bunker would just cancel all welfare and food stamps, and "everybody" would just have to "get off their dead ass." While this method would eliminate the abuses, there are folks that are trying, but they just need some help. Stan supports this. Mindful of the girl gangs in the city alleys, Stan realizes that there are foster parents out there that are just running a puppy mill for the money. Stan's heart breaks for the kids in this situation. But Stan reflects. While he wasn't abused as a child, his upbringing was not exactly conventional. He owes "his success" to a strong work ethic, which his father instilled in him. So when Stan has these moments with others children, he tries to show them that there is a way, if you're willing to work.

Stan reflects that America is far ahead of other countries in this regard. Stan has worked in the United Kingdom with non-Americans. As it is a social country, there really is no incentive to work. Basically, the low skilled labor jobs pay about the same as unemployment, so why work? Most only do until they qualify for unemployment, or disability.

In other countries Stan has experienced "servant" cultures in which the labor is not paid. Their family all live on the work grounds, in separate housing, sometimes just a hay barn, but their food, medical requirements, etc are met by the "patron". Usually in the servant structure there is no formal education, so many of these populations cannot read or write.

As with all things people, Stan has reflected on the Indians. Some are just like the "social" Brit's, in that there is no incentive to work. Others are very driven for different reasons, but seldom for financial gain. They do it to help their people. So everybody is different, all over the world.

The Indians are very charitable to their own. Basically, if there is a need, the word spreads, and while the need may not be fully met, nobody starves to death.

Stan is all over the board on charity, and does not consider it to necessarily constitute a financial contribution. Sometimes it is donating your time that makes a difference. Stan's employer was big on supporting food banks. Stan has witnessed this first hand. The folks needing food did not fit in one demographic. It was all over the board, from elderly white women to teenage blacks.

Stan will not tell you what is right or wrong, or what to do. First, he would suggest that you reflect on your desires, and consider anything that dovetails to that. This will be the easiest for you, and bring you the most satisfaction. So this could be a modest financial contribution, say five bucks, or it could be a tax altering threshold of hundreds or even thousands. As stated, it may be time, like giving rides to medical appointments. In regards to donating time, Stan would have you construct a "time budget" in that you physically list where you "spend" your time. This is different than a financial budget. There are no rich or poor people. Everybody is allotted the same amount of time, worldwide; twenty four hours every seven days a week.

Stan warns you to be careful. An automatic for Stan is animal shelters, but he has tried it and it depressed him. Stan knows you can't have feral dogs and cats roaming the neighborhood. He has seen children attacked by "wild dogs" firsthand on his garbage route. On one occasion he took a small boy to the ER that was bitten in the face by a Doberman pinscher. Stan could see the child's teeth and tongue through his cheek sitting in the passenger seat. The police found the dog, and shot it. They hauled it to the dump. Stan realizes that there has to be some system, and he readily admits that he does not have the answers, but he just can't be around animals destined for the dump in thirty days. His forty acres just isn't big enough, and he already has twenty animals. So your charity may be right for you, donating yarn to the nursing home for the knitters, and even knitting with them. Just reflect, very seriously.

While your desire may be what you hold in your heart, you don't want your charity to hurt anyone, especially you. One thing that Stan and his wife have done is simply different things every time with no rhyme or reason. Stan learned this from his wife. She had a coworker that was a very nice young gal. She was an office staff person, which are surprisingly low paid in the medical profession. This gal had three children, was separated from an abusive husband, and was just struggling. Christmas was coming soon. While she did not whine or complain to anyone, Stan's wife recognized the concern. She asked Stan if he minded helping her, and Stan said no, do what you want. She placed three one hundred dollar bills in the persons work station where she would find it, no note, no nothing. This was out of her hay sales stash.

The young gal ran around the clinic asking if anyone knew who did this. Nobody knew, but that entire clinic had a merry Christmas for three hundred bucks. So if you're into the charity for the tax deduction, or recognition, this isn't for you. If you want to see co-workers smile, Stan's sure you have one; "just open your heart".

Stan has found poor people to be the most giving. Christmas is a huge ceremony for Hispanics. One town Stan's company serves is ninety percent Hispanics, mostly transient Ag labor, so they're not in the same place year to year. It's not like they've known "Fred" all of their life. But this route got so many gifts the week before Christmas that they literally rented a storage unit because they would get more each day than they could carry in the cab of the truck. When poor people give gifts to the garbage man that they don't know, we're not talking hundred dollar bills.

Stan would help these two men haul their booty back to the shop in his pick-up. It was all over the board, from a can of corn to a fifth of tequila. Sometimes there was a card with cash, never over ten dollars. Sometimes it was food like a cooked turkey, chicken, or smoked pork. Stan reflected that the guys that served the poorest neighborhoods got the most stuff. The guys that served the rich neighborhoods got their ass chewed for being late because it had snowed two feet.

So Stan suggests just to do what calls to your heart. There is no right or wrong. Don't extend yourself and risk your own families livelihood, but whatever you do will brighten someone, or somethings day.

V: The phone call. This technology has changed many times in Stan's life, and before. It used to be a telegram prior to Stan's birth. That's how you found out your son or husband was dead in Germany in World War One or Two. Nobody much has a home phone line anymore, actually for a telephone. Now any hard wiring is probably for a computer, which is also your "cable" TV.

Stan's first telephone experiences were actually a "party line", not to suggest that there was any party, but folks shared the same line, so you could pick up the phone and listen to someone else's conversation. You had to wait for them to finish before you called anyone. Of course cellular service has changed the phone call worldwide.

What this topic suggests is receiving that shock bit of news about some major event. When this news is sprung upon you, good, or usually bad, this is a time to reflect. The days of the telegram were probably more accommodating to reflection because all you had was a piece of paper some kid left at the door. There was nothing to react at.

You can prepare yourself for the bad news. One of the most common that Stan has witnessed is when someone's final parent passes away. This creates a level of loneliness for most. You always had that "safe" place to return to. Now you are on your own, even though you have been for thirty years. All those "things you should have done" or "said" flood your mind. You are alone now.

As with all definitions by category, The Phone Call could be under the Heartbreak, Death, or others depending on the details. It does not have to be a phone call. It could be the letter, or what Stan calls an "oh, by the way" as someone drops a bomb on you verbally. For Stan "the call" was actually a story in a newspaper about a barn burning down with twenty horses inside. For someone that tragedy would fall under Financial.

It does not matter. As you reflect on your life, these possibilities that don't happen are a cause for celebration of your heart. If you have a relative or friend in the military you can reflect that they have come to no harm. That could be today, tomorrow, or at the end of their enlistment. There are all kinds of military circumstances. Someone that hijacks a jet and fly's it into a skyscraper is committing an act of war. Even if it is not an official declaration from a foreign country carried out by their military people, attacking masses with no warning by a terrorist is an act of war.

Reflect that that could happen to any of us, anytime, and appreciate what little that you may have, or don't have. Never take anything for granted. Never abuse anything, as an example water, just because you can. Water is precious. Water gives and sustains life. If you have more than enough, that does not mean that you should use more than you need. Just reflect that you appreciate having more than you need, and let the next person have it. Don't react when they waste the water that you sent them. Reflect, separate your brain from your heart, smile, breathe, and walk away, let it go. As Mr. T would say "I pity the fool!"

Stan has a life full of memorable "calls". He remembers when his grandfather died, and his dad got that call. He can remember his father's reaction when they heard that John F Kennedy had been assassinated in Dallas Texas from a radio in the cab of a dump truck his dad was driving. Both of his ex-wives had dropped a bomb on him.

In the end, life goes on. Don't allow bad news to poison your heart. That does not mean that you are indifferent, or don't care. But separate the digestion of the news from your brain thinking it through, from your heart. As a human experiences life, he collects these bad circumstances. Life does not heal all wounds. Some things just are not supposed to happen. A parent should not outlive their children. But sometimes they do. Reflect that you are grateful, and appreciate the times that you shared. If you have accepted mortality in your heart, you realize that anything is possible. Like water, don't take anyone's energy for granted.

One of Stan's reasons for being agnostic, is because he reflects that a good God would not allow certain atrocities to occur. Stan does not blame God. There are many ways people deal with these sad issues; some use religion, or family, or friends. For a student it may be a teacher that they look up to. For an employee it may be their boss. Reflect; for someone it may be you. Being strong in the face of brutality is a religious act in itself. Once it is in the past, it can't be changed. Change what you can moving forward, but as far as your heart is concerned, the past stays in the past. Reflect on moving forward. That's what you can influence.

W: The Report Card. There is a reason that Stan doesn't have a category on raising children. That would be its own book with subsections on raising others children. The report card is that moment that somebody criticized your little buttercup. Your child, which is God's gift to the planet in your mind, got a D or F in a class with a comment like "needs to keep hands to herself".

Wow! This is a good time to reflect. First off, why didn't you hear about this before now? The person determining this grade and comment is an educated professional. They are only trying to help in the development of your child. Stan's example is math. It has always been dead easy for Stan, and he cannot understand why it isn't for his daughter. Of course the way that they teach math has changed since Stan was in school, but his daughter just does not comprehend the subject. And what's this about her hands? Stan finds out in a parent teacher conference that his little buttercup is a bully, and shoves people around.

Stan's first instinct is to react. As he reflects on his possible reactions, what good would spanking or grounding the child do? Stan reflects that she needs more love. More math at home, and less TV. Stan needs to pay attention to her friends, and talk to her about touching other people, uninvited. Stan reflects that it is not her fault, that it is his fault for not paying attention. STAN SAYS: "why do they call it paying attention? You don't pay anyone anything".

This is the same as The Phone Call in that it is bad news that totally blind sides you. You aren't expecting it. It is just a shot out of the blue sky. Whether it's The Report Card or The Phone Call, Stan reflects that you just have to open both your mind and your heart to any eventuality. Opening your mind to any eventuality is harder than most recognize in themselves. Almost everyone has preconceived ideas' about how things work in the world. It gets a little narrower when it's your little buttercup and you consider yourself a good parent.

One way that Stan reacts to the unanticipated is to reflect on any event that he hears about, whether that is a jetliner crash, an auto accident, or other tragedy that does not involve anyone that he knows when he hears or sees it on the news, in the paper, or on the radio. Stan is grateful that nobody he knows was involved, and he realizes that it could someday. Stan wishes all involved, alive or dead, whatever their beliefs held in their hearts, to come true.

Stan has reflected that a bad grade is not the end of the world, and that the United States education system is substandard compared to many parts of the world. Still, his daughter needs to try, and at least reach a C in math. Stan has seen successful careers develop for folks that did not necessarily do well in public school.

Stan reflects that his daughter cannot be allowed to be a bully, and have a content life. He considers sports such as karate or judo, where discipline is a component of the sport. Reaction with reflection. The only reason people become bully's is because that has worked for them. It would be good for her to know there are others that can kick her butt, maybe smaller and younger than her.

So whatever the "bomb" surprise may be, Stan suggests reflection from all angles. Once you have reflected all the angles, develop your reaction around what is in the best interest for everyone involved. There is no "win". There is only making the attempt. Allowing the daughter her input in this example is crucial. This is not an argument. You have to calmly hear them out.

X. The Nightmares. Stan does not have nightmares. He doesn't even have dreams unless it is something he was thinking about when he fell asleep. Stan's wife has nightmares regularly. So as all things human, everyone is different, For Stan and his wife the bed is the same, the temperature of the room is the same, their dog sleeps between them, they share financial and family circumstances, everything else is the same, yet they are totally different in regards to nightmares. Stan reflects that this is common in life; that everyone is different, yet everything is the same.

As Stan reflects the why of his wife's nightmares, he feels that he does a "better", or more thorough job of thinking things through, and he is not as emotional, which Stan has discovered women can be, over men. Stan reflects on the why. First off, her job is very stressful, sometimes literally life and death. Stan's is so simple that he actually sometimes does it "in his sleep". Stan has offered to have her quit, but rather hesitantly. The job that she does so well is unnoticed, but vital to the health of the community. There might be two other people qualified to perform her job functions within a hundred mile radius. Stan does not want to "steal" his wife from the community.

They discuss her nightmares and the cause. Often they are so fragmented that you just cannot make any sense of it. Stan has experienced other religions. He compares this unintelligible scenario to folks that "speak in tongues". Following such an episode, they cannot explain exactly what happened, even if they watch a video of themselves doing it, they just have a more relaxed feeling about life.

So Stan reflects that in some way his wife's nightmares could be a religious experience. They share a common question of religions, and any "hereafter". Stan suggests that if you suffer nightmares, reflect on it. Sometimes having a pencil and paper next to the bed so that you can right down any thoughts helps to recover the episode when you awaken. Stan's wife's nightmares are so vivid she wakes up in a full sweat, and breathing hard, but she cannot remember any details. Once in a while she can recall a person, maybe a coworker, but it has no bearing on anything.

Stan has broken his brain, and does have some experience with mental health. When someone's brain is sheared, they do not have any "automatic" body controls, like holding your pee until you make it to the potty. A person can control their breathing and respiration. So if you get excited, and your heart rate and respiration climb, you can relax yourself mentally, and maybe walk around and stretch to relieve the stress. A person with a sheared brain has no body controls. Indeed, many die from "panic attacks" in which their heart rate and respiration climb so out of control that their heart or arteries explode.

Stan has discovered that some folks are prone to panic attacks, and just cannot control their heart rate. They get prescription drugs to calm them down. Others have the opposite issue and need anti-depressant's to survive. Stan has been on these drugs, and does not like the mental feeling.

Stan would suggest that if you are reflective about literally everything, even the idiot that doesn't merge correctly getting on the freeway, that you will avoid the nightmare. But that requires discipline. Almost nobody merges correctly. Being reflective requires you to think through every single situation, even, and especially, the one's that you cannot control.

Stan and his wife have reflected on her nightmares at length. Stan's guess is that she has so much stimuli in a given day, that she just cannot process everything, much less reflect on every item. Stan feels regret that there is nothing he can do to relieve her nightmares. She actually has psychiatrists and neurologists that work for her, so health care access is not the issue. They have discovered that hot yoga, with Buddhist undertones, help more than anything else, exercise with spiritual reflection. She has dabbled in acupuncture, and gains some stress relief from that. This is a woman in professional medical care getting relief from "unconventional" alternatives. Stan reflects that you don't know unless you open your mind and try it. STAN SAYS: "nothing ventured, nothing gained".

Y. Garbage Day. STAN SAYS: "we can't pick it up if you hide it". Referring to someone that forgot to put their cans out on garbage day. This segment also involves Transportation, and is actually about scheduling your life's events. Stan refers to this scheduling as garbage day, because that is a mistake that you make once, then make a conscious effort not to ever forget again.

So this scheduling of you life's events depends on who you are, where you are, and your responsibilities in life. If you pick your teenage daughter up after varsity basketball practice, then that is daily except for Sunday. She practices every afternoon after school, and has a game on Friday and Saturday nights. Either way, home game or away, you have to drop her off at the high school, either for the home game, or to catch the bus to the away games, which you then drive to. Of course there is dinner to work into the schedule. These daily schedules aren't hard to remember because they are daily, just like work.

Where you are changes everything. Generally, on the west coast, everyone drives a car. This takes in expenses such a gas. That may not be the case on the east coast. Many people don't own a car. So these responsibilities may determine your home location. If you live in a large east coast city you may move to "the burbs" and have a longer commute to work yourself. Stan reflects that many families have no such option available, and simply have to raise their children in "inner city" schools, and use public transportation. The quality of these schools vary from one to the next, so your teenage daughter's school may determine where you live, which may determine where you work.

Stan reflects that everything in your life is interrelated in a scheduling sort of way. If you consider "time is money" as in getting paid by the hour, then scheduling your time for both personal interests, work, and a loved one's safety, is "spending" your time, which is your limited lifetime on earth. This requires a budget similar to your finances. Of course there is no way to "bank" time. The clock ticks, and when your time is up, it's up. Everyone on earth gets the same sixty minutes per hour, twenty-four times each day.

So reflect; are you spending two hours a day parked on a freeway in rush hour traffic? That is probably a good time to floss your teeth. Stan has studied plans that some cities have considered to disconnect themselves from the freeway grid. There would be no commuting to the city from the burbs. You both live and work in the city, or you do not. Not every scheduled event is a garbage day, or daily such as work or basketball practice. Some are bi-annual, such as dentist's appointments. Stan keeps his on a calendar at his work because he needs to request the time off, and have someone cover for him at the dump. Of course it's on Face book; "Stan's at the dentist".

While we're on Face book, many now do their life's schedule on their phone. Stan thinks that's fine, but just like texting or Face booking, don't do it while you're driving. Pull over. A lot of garbage men get hit by folks looking at their I phone.

As you're busy doing all this scheduling, or "putting the trash out the night before garbage day" as Stan would say, Stan recommends that you reflect on what you want to "spend" your time doing. You only have so many days on this side of the grass. What are your passions? May be that you simply get up from in front of your flat screen, and go play with your dog. Or you get that second part time job and save that pay for that once in a lifetime travel vacation.

Stan reflects that most of your time "putting the trash out" is actually a reaction to the things that you have put in motion, maybe unconsciously. So just like a financial budget, write out a time budget, and where you "spend" it. Then absorb it, and reflect for several days. There may be some things that you eliminate. Write in some wishes. It's your time, your life. You spend it all, but doing what?

STAN SAYS: "you're wasting heartbeats that I can never get back" to some unarmed mental soldier that is attempting to bait him into a battle of wits, and "in some cultures that's considered murder". So reflect; if you have people that are stealing your heart beats for no good reason, then you are allowing them to murder you. Don't do it. Stan's wife worked with a person with a last name of "Smalls". It became a common phrase in the medical community; "you're killing me Smalls!"

So the next time you put the trash out, mentally put the scheduled items that don't serve you out with them. Leave it in the past. You can't change yesterday, all that you have control of is you moving forward. Stan does not suggest impulse reactions, but rather well reflected choices.

FINANCES

A: Business. STAN SAYS: "If your drift exceeds your draft, you've definitely run aground". Stan feels this accurately describes the monetary system, in your personal life, in your country, in the world. Stan has been in other countries where the locals have no money. They have never had money. There is nothing to buy. Whether you are a servant in India, a native in central Mexico, or an Arab out in the Sahara Desert.

Americans cannot fathom such a life. Indeed, in these other cultures your day is "spent" gathering food and maintaining some kind of shelter from the elements. This does not mean a nice house with a yard. It could be an old abandoned junk vehicle, or a "structure" built from pallets, or a hole in the ground. There is no arguing over what will be watched on Netflix. There is no complaining of cell phone "bars". Of course the lifespan is much shorter. As Stan reflects on these cultures, he begins to understand extremist organizations. That is not to say that he condones violence, murder, or terrorism such as flying jets into high rise buildings. He does not. "Live and let live" as a murdered John Lennon would sing. But an extremist sect that has literally nothing to live for accepts "Armageddon" as an improvement in their being. They will be a martyr, and remembered for something great.

But as Stan reflects on such things, what would Americans do if they had a "substandard" living in abject poverty? A lot of the folks Stan came to know were actually quite happy in their lives. They weren't worried about starving; they had reliable food sources, even though there was no shopping in stores. They had no stress, such as getting fired, work deadlines, overdrawn accounts, or the power getting shut off. They had accepted mortality because there is little or no modern health care, so death was common in their culture. They usually had some religious belief, thankful for everything good; family, friends, weather, water. Stan reflects that hardly describes a typical American.

So Stan is fine driving his old beater Nissan an hour each way to his job running the Indians dump. He is even grateful. Sure he likes nice vehicles, but he doesn't want a car payment. His Visa card limit is fifty thousand dollars, and his credit score is nine hundred, so he can buy whatever he wants. His peace of mind is worth more than all that junk. He raises his own food even though it costs more than buying the items on sale, or online. He reflects that he and his wife eat better than anyone else they know, and he is grateful for that. Their favorite activity is giving their children food.

Stan used to chase the golden goose. One of his original mentors owned a garbage company that he worked for. This guy was of Jewish decent, and flaunted his wealth; two Pantera sports cars (why would anyone need two?), a Humvee, boats, lots of toys. He did not wear fancy clothes; just comfortable jeans and T-shirts. As Stan was in his twenties at this time, and mechanically inclined, this lifestyle impressed him. But the man had a lot of financial pressure to maintain his lifestyle. As Stan became reflective, he realized that this literally was the man's reason for living, and it made Stan sad. He liked this man, even though nobody else did, but that he did not appreciate "the little things".

His next employer was exactly the opposite. Stan reflects that that is what made the change in him. The stark comparison of one financial philosophy to another.

This man was of Italian decent, which is its own microcosm culture of the mainstream. He had bought a financially troubled garbage company a hundred miles away, and hired Stan to run it because; Stan was raised in the region and knew it well, and Stan had a reputation as a damned good garbage man. The previous owner had run the company into the ground financially. He was a heavy gambler at the racehorse track. Indeed that's where they met and did the deal, because Stan's new boss ran a string of race horses too. But Stan witnessed firsthand the disciplined business approach to operating an expensive hobby. The seller was flat broke, but lived in a fancy house and drove a new Cadillac.

Stan's first day on the job, he drove his Ford Bronco up to the front gate, which was closed and locked. Stan thought Huh? These routes should have started several hours ago. The drivers were picketing. The previous owner had docked their wages for financial reasons, and had promised reimbursement and back wages. The driver's reckoned it was get it right when it sold, or never see a dime. This was probably the time in life when Stan became reflective. This was not his first rodeo. This was the first time that he was the boss, and responsible.

Stan had been around many garbage company strikes. He knew that they were emotional on both sides. In a previous strike under his previous boss, he had pulled twenty two "jacks" out of a flat front tire. The strikers where driving ahead of the routes throwing out the toy "land mines". Of course, in true American press coverage, the front page story showed the striking men "teaching" the replacement scabs the routes; yeah, right. But Stan reflected on what his reaction should be.

Stan went downtown, bought two dozen maple bars, and twenty cups of coffee, and drove back to his front gate. He backed up to the picketers, dropped his Bronco tailgate, and sat there and chatted with the men. He was upfront with all of them, and couldn't answer their questions, because he just didn't know what the future would bring. He asked their opinions. He couldn't comment on the previous owner being an asshole, because he just did not know the man, but it was obvious to him that something was wrong. Stan promised to do the best that he could for them, that he was a garbage man too. No he did not know the new owner, this was his first day. The reason the gate was closed and locked was not the strike. None of the drivers' could unlock it. The IRS had seized the property and put their chain and lock on the gate for unpaid taxes.

It got worse. The County had closed the garbage company's account at the landfill due to delinquency. Stan reflected that it's pretty hard to collect garbage once all the trucks are full and there's nowhere to dump. STAN SAYS: "a full truck is the same as no truck".

Stan contacted his new owner and gave him the short version of the events. His owner told him to keep a diary, that he would overnight checks to Stan's motel room to cover the expenses, that it was going to be the same with the fuel guy, tire guy, everybody.

Stan could not believe how calm and relaxed this man was over very serious matters owning a garbage company. Stan's previous boss would have looked like the Space Shuttle blowing up. The next day Fed Ex showed up at the motel with ten checks. Stan went to the IRS and paid the previous owners unpaid taxes, some two hundred thousand dollars. Then he went to the County and brought the landfill account current, three hundred thousand dollars. He took doughnuts to the drivers, and as the IRS unlocked the gate, he said he would do what he could, and they all went back to work. The rest of the week went that way; the fuel guy, the telephone company, the billing invoice printer. The ten checks were gone.

Stan's new owner came over the following week, with more checks. He sat Stan down and told him to go easy; that there was money held back from the seller anticipating this. He would deduct these expenses from the withheld funds, which would result in a lawsuit; that he was responsible for all the debts once Stan drove up to the gate the first time, and he would pay all of his bills at net ten days.

This truly made a lifelong impression on Stan. This man held no stress. Million dollar problems did not faze him. This is not to say that he was not emotional, he was, in true Italian ancestry. He couldn't talk without waving his arms. But his emotion was over how good the server was, or how bad the cook was. The money was just business. STAN SAYS: "once we started answering the phone and picking up the garbage, the business took off". Of course to an outsider that's a duh for a garbage company, or as STAN SAYS: "business stinks" and "the business is picking up".

In the end the drivers got their back wages, and their raise, retroactive as the seller had promised, and the funds came out of the money held back by the buyer. They even went non-union as the buyer provided better medical, dental, and life insurance than what the union had, and there were no dues. Stan was truly impressed by this man's business acumen. He was not some pedigreed businessman; he was just an old time Italian garbage man. STAN SAYS: "money is not complicated, people make money complicated".

Stan has reflected on money. He had worked in Great Britain. The British had discontinued using the one pound note several years prior to Stan's arrival, with several years notice to its citizens'. Anything under a five pound note moving forward would be a coin. It's funny how people stash money; in piggy banks, rolled up under the refrigerator, wherever. But Stan learned the hard way, as he received a lot of one pound paper notes as change from the gas station, restaurant, everywhere; until he was switched on that they were worthless. STAN SAYS: "those lessons you learn the hard way are the ones that you remember". In true hoarder mentality, Stan still has British one pound notes squirreled away in his stash. He just can't bring himself to throw them away.

But Stan does reflect on money with his Indian garbage customers. Of course, in the beginning, the Indians had no money, and traded or bartered for items, or confiscated them in a raid attack on another tribe.

Once the white man came along, they were exposed to money, mostly silver and gold, but they continued to barter. Once currency came along, they did not believe in the government backing the value of the paper. It got worse with Confederate or territory currencies. So generally, the Indians traded for furs, foods, or handmade items.

The Indians land is not a private parcel as with non-Indian ownership. The Indian lands are either tribal trust or allotments in which the Indians are allowed to live there, and work the land tax free. But they cannot get financing on the property as the lender cannot foreclose on tribal land, making the land useless, monetarily. The Indians get a small monthly stipend from the tribe. Many attempt to live off of this stipend on allotment land, but it is nowhere near enough to survive in a healthy lifestyle in today's economy. Stan just observes and reflects, without judgment. These Indians just blow through their stipend like a drunken sailor on shore leave. It's almost like they consider the money worthless, like Stan's British one pound notes, and just get whatever they can with it. In that regard, just like the graffitti'ed dumpsters, it is a form of economic development, in a way.

Every so many years, perhaps three or four times a generation, the Indians get some "settlement" from the US Government. This is usually some significant amount, several thousand dollars, for some slight or wrong doing in the past. Sometimes it is not even for Stan's reservations tribe, it is a "class action" from a lawsuit somewhere else with some other Indians. Back when Stan was reactive, he was just like most Americans, disagreeing with using his tax dollars to give a handout to the Indians. But as Stan became reflective, his thought processes changed. Stan reckons that this is how Rosie bought her Escalade.

Stan has researched it some. The way the United States treated the native peoples was atrocious; akin to Hitler's Nazi Germany and the Jews. Stan's little local tribe had the Indian children torn from their homes and sent to "Agency" schools where they had their long hair sheared, where refused to speak in their local tongue and beat if they did not use English, and worked in shops eight hours a day with a couple more hours of class to read, write, and do math. The United States figured this was the best way to "change" the tribes. It figured the adults were beyond "saving".

Indeed, as Stan researched it, he discovered that President Lincoln's "Emancipation Proclamation" "granted" the native populations the same rights as other Americans, as it did the freed slaves. Stan reflected on it. At what point are all of the historical issues settled? Ever? Can the atrocities be reversed? Does money accomplish that? Just like the graffitti'ed dumpsters or the blown stipends, these settlements are gone within days if not hours, which makes it a type of economic development. The car dealers, big screen TV shops, furniture stores, appliance stores, all benefit almost immediately from these settlements. There is little or no thought to saving for the future, college tuitions', or a rainy day. Stan reflects that it is a "live for now" mentality from a culture that never really valued money, and was nearly annihilated from the face of the earth. This is the seventh generation of welfare going back to the treaty, which was forced on them. STAN SAYS: "one generation of poverty raising the next generation leads to a trap that the victims cannot break the cycle of".

Stan reflected these finances, and how he would have reviewed it from his reactive youth. If you would have asked him if he supported the United States "giving" the Indians fifty one billion dollars, his response would have been "hell no". Stan reflected that if you asked the U.S. Chamber of Commerce if they supported spreading fifty one billion dollars across the auto, furniture, and appliance industries, that they would probably support it, with the qualification of which auto, furniture, and appliances were to be purchased.

Upon further reflection, Stan compared it to the military. This tribe's treaty was tied to the impending Civil War. The North did not want an enemy at their back while they were fighting the South, and they did not want the Indians aiding the Rebels. So they threw fourteen bands and tribes together and took eleven million acres from them, and forced them onto their "Reserve".

Stan reflects that in all reality, this is still an extension of that military act, which was the Treaty. Stan reflects that fifty one billion dollars to the American military is simply a rounding error, and a drop in the bucket. This "settlement" is no different than the military America still supports in Korea, Germany, the Middle East, and Japan. At least Rosie spent her settlement at a local Cadillac dealer, which supports jobs that shop at Wal Mart, Safeway, etc.

So Stan runs both his work and personal financials the same way the Italian owner had shown him. Stan says: "money is simple, it's people that make money complicated". As an example to the different mentalities, Stan would offer that he ran a large company for twenty years, very successfully, with no profit and loss statement (P&L). His owner expected him to know every revenue stream to the dollar; paper, pens, diesel, band aids. This owner knew all the percentages of income for any "line item" such as labor, fuel, or dump fee to a profitable garbage company. The garbage business was regulated in this state meaning that the company was audited by the state, and a "fair" rate was allowed for operating a good, safe company; in essence, a regulated monopoly.

Stan's owner would invest several million dollars in new trucks and containers. The drivers all got substantial raises. The salary could not be outside of "the local norm" but it could be at the high end, which attracts good help. Benefits such as dependent insurance coverage or employer retirement contributions were allowed. Stan's owner showed him that you load the allowed expenses up front, get a good rate approved, and then "run lean" for five to seven years, and then do it again. This company would clear twenty percent, even though ten percent profit was the maximum allowed, for five or six years, and then begin "losing" money. They would reinvest, and start all over again. This required a lot of discipline. It made Stan think ahead about five years, basically, for what he wanted. After that he was stuck with his decision. STAN SAYS: "plan your work, and work your plan". They had over two million dollars in a pass book checking account that didn't even draw any interest. When Stan questioned his owner about it, the reply was "don't worry about it, I might want to buy something."

Several of these government accounts required significant bonding capacity for liability. Stan's owner would just have him buy a certificate of deposit (CD) for the amount required, and have the government entity and the garbage company named as signers on the CD. STAN SAYS: "buying bonding is betting against yourself" or "put your money where your mouth is".

When this owner died and his children sold the company, Stan got a taste of the corporate world. They had a value. They defined integrity as; "say what you are going to do, and then do it". Which sounded fantastic to Stan. But then he witnessed the application. This national publicly traded company required a monthly financial forecast for the next month. Then they followed it with a "mid-month" adjustment two weeks later. Of course there were requirements that you had to meet to get "your" P&L accepted. It's pretty hard to tell at the end of November how much snow you will get in December. Stan has two decades of experience here. Some years its zero, and other years its four feet in two days. If you didn't hit "your number" which was actually corporates number, you were accused of "taking an integrity vacation". As this happened post brain shear, Stan just didn't give a damn any more. One example is fuel. Folks have a general idea that it goes up and down regularly. Stan was very in tune as he had a ten thousand gallon fuel tank, and filled it every ten days. His fuel vendor and he became friends. Stan was his biggest account. He questioned the large construction companies and the school buses. His vendor told him; Yeah, they use a lot, but you're the only steady account year around. The construction company doesn't run in winter, and the school buses don't run in summer.

This concept stuck with Stan. He got a very good price because the vendor appreciated his business, and he paid net ten days. When the national company bought them all the CD's were cashed in. They bought their fuel on "futures" predictions, which saved money nationally, but it was more than Stan was paying locally. Of course there was no net ten days, that flew out the window with the CD's. Stan's previous owner would watch the price of fuel like a hawk. It was not unusual for Fred Meyers to have diesel cheaper than what Stan had just bought ten thousand gallons for, so all the garbage trucks fueled at Fred Meyers until the price went up a nickel. Stan learned that it's the little things that matter. STAN SAYS: "don't worry about the dollars, they'll take care of themselves, worry about the pennies". At the next rate filing following the sale of the company, Stan got a nine percent rate reduction. Not only was it embarrassing, it was unheard of, and very unprofessional. That was the last straw. Nice enough people, but STAN SAYS: "no brains, no headaches".

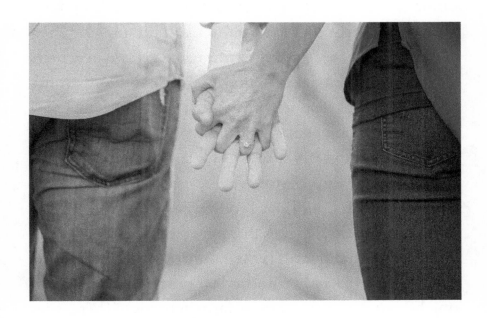

B: Personal. Stan admits openly that his wife is better at their personal finances than he is. She has lived through some rough times, and scrambled to put food on the table for her kids. Stan admires that. Stan's only rough times were when he was a child living with his father. There was no extra money, but his dad worked three jobs, so there was never any vacations or weekend holidays. Stan's wife actually makes more money than Stan, as his previous two wives did. Stan tries not to blow through "her" money. He tries to live within his salary. They have a very nice property with good farm equipment, a nice big barn, and a newer home. She enjoys the property very much. So their biggest expense is probably all their animals. They hardly ever go out to dinner. They raise their own food and prefer that to a restaurant.

Stan's idea of a shopping extravaganza is two new pairs of bib overalls. He used to make junkets to Nordstrom's twice a year, but he doesn't miss that. He has some holey (not religious holy) socks and underwear that he refuses to throw away. STAN SAYS: "I'm easy to shop for".

Stan has no bills beyond fuel to get to work, farming supplies, utilities, and pet food. His wife drives a nice, newer car, and Stan makes that payment. Their forty acres with the house and farm is their only expense. Stan wants to die on his place, but not today. He reflects as to how long he can do all the various farm activities. There is no answer. It's month to month and year to year. Worst case scenario, he leases out the hay.

Stan has reflected that nobody wants to hire a sixty plus year old has-been. The Indians are probably the only ones that will have him. He knows that he is worth far more in the private sector doing what he does, but he likes the laid back atmosphere "on the Rez", and he knows the Tribe will never sell. Stan supports his wife's efforts, which are considerable running a multi-million dollar health care facility. He readily admits that he doesn't know boo about running Doc's or the changing dynamics of the payer mix with Medicare, Medicaid, and private insurance, but he tutors her on knowing her P&L inside and out; what the revenue streams are both ways, and if you subsidize a loser, why? Stan guides her on the little things. As mentioned throughout this book, a lot of business theft is in house. It's no different at the garbage company or the clinic. Of course no one steals the garbage, but there's the toilet paper, pens, paper, printer cartridges, oil filters, on and on. Stan looks at the accounts receivables, every day. At the clinic there are med's, surgery supplies, even rock salt for the walkways in winter.

Stan has shown his wife that to circumvent this, as well as embezzlement, separate the various duties. Have everyone get their office supplies from one person, we'll call her Cindy. If Debbie needs two hundred pens a month and everyone else gets by with two, why? Cindy approves ALL invoices for payment, and has the details memorized. The same person that picks up the mail does not open it. The person that opens it does not do the deposit, and the person that deposits the checks does not key the payments to the accounts. She must look at the accounts receivable every day, and she'll have the seasonal cycle of an Ag labor economy down.

So this has gone back to business finances, but that's how Stan and his wife live their lives. STAN SAYS: "if you don't have a paying job, leave your credit card in your wallet". Stan and his wife tend to "squirrel" some money away, just for fun. Stan gives her the cash for what little hay he sells. It varies from five hundred to two thousand dollars a year. It is never questioned. They just blow it however they wish. They dribble a little out to help their kids, and Stan gives his daughter ten thousand dollars a year for tuition. The rest is up to her, and she has a part time job. Once every year or two they buy a horse, which runs five to ten thousand dollars. They do not have a formal budget. They just have the two payments; car and property, and they each get paid every two weeks on offset cycles, so they have all the money they want, but don't consider themselves rich.

Their retirement accounts are now invested in "secure" funds which don't grow as fast, but they are conservative, and they both realize that the American economy is overdue to collapse. Stan reflects that the other countries that he as visited will both catch up, and move ahead, or the United States will decline, and fall behind. Stan views the American education system as both poor quality, and out dated.

C: Cash flow. This subject is so simple, but Stan reflects that nobody gets it. Again, his Italian garbage company owner drilled this into his head. That's why he had two million dollars in a passbook checking account; in case he wanted to buy something. Americans tend to spend forward, with money due before they even get paid. Stan considers payday loans to be criminal, and feels that they should be banned. Stan has loaned several hundred garbage men a hundred bucks on a Monday when payday was the following Friday, to buy gas for their pick-up, diapers, bread, milk, and beer.

Of course Stan reflects on the Indians. They tend to have a "live for today" mentality with no concern for the future. He hears several brag about how they hit it big at "their" casino, like they have some inside track, but they don't brag about how many times they drop everything in five minutes and walk out broke. STAN SAYS: "there's a reason that they don't close and the lights are always on".

So if you are struggling financially, Stan offers this suggestion; Take a piece of paper and a pencil and write down all of your monthly expenses by category; food, travel, entertainment, housing, utilities. If you have a bi-annual bill such as auto insurance, convert it to a monthly amount. What you should end up with is a years living expenses broken into twelve monthly amounts. Next take a calendar and place the dollar amount of any income that you have on that date for that month.

Then match your payments due to the corresponding paycheck. If you're rent is due on the first, you pay it with your check on the twenty eighth. This is cash flow. This exercise will give you an opportunity to reflect on how necessary some of your expenses are. There may be some hard choices to make. Saying no to yourself isn't as much fun as binge buying.

Stan recommends that you have two months expenses saved, outside of retirement plans. Stan struggles to stay within this limit. Six months would be better, but let's get to two months first. You could break your brain any day falling down some stairs, or stepping off a sidewalk curb. Now you're talking seven years!

Stan doesn't recommend cutting expenses immediately as most are probably thinking. Stan figures you gotta live your life. Stan suggests that you increase your income. This doesn't mean asking your boss for a raise or stealing toilet paper to set up a sidewalk stand. This means getting a part time job, maybe just for a couple months. But as you are a cashier at a Seven Eleven, or some other job, your priorities will shine through. Maybe you don't need that fancy I-pad plan. Maybe you don't need that I-pad. There are more cell phones than flushing toilets on planet earth, so Stan won't suggest that, but there are a lot of folks that don't have a cell phone, and have a lot of stress-less free time.

Build your two month, or even six month pad. Once the financial discipline takes root, just stick to your plan. Do not get a payday loan or some other high interest scam, like a reverse mortgage. Just kick yourself in the butt like a heroin addict has to, to quit cold turkey. Getting a loan from friends or family doesn't do any good, it's just another bill that needs to be paid. YOU must balance your expenses to your income. It doesn't matter what other people have. This is about you. Skip the sale at the clothing store. Don't order anything on line. A good lesson in cash flow is to actually go back to old school, pay in cash. If you don't have the cash, you don't buy it. Stan reflects that it does not get any simpler than that.

D: Self-employed. Stan has done this a few times, but does not recommend himself as a "how to" example. Stan considers himself more of a "what not to do" example. STAN SAYS: "when you make your hobby your job, it just isn't fun anymore".

Stan has had his own company three times in his life, not counting his hay farming operation. Two of these were metal fabrication businesses, specializing in, what else, garbage collection equipment. The other was a consulting company for garbage collection and disposal operations. Stan has witnessed other people make a go of these businesses, but it just was not for Stan. To begin, Stan quit his jobs at the garbage companies to run his enterprises. But his largest by far, and sometimes only customer was the garbage company that he left, so basically he was just doing his old job, but had all the taxes, benefits, Labor and Industries, and other headaches that he never did himself as the manager. Stan hates this work. The financial offset was about the same. At the end of the day he was clearing about what he did running the garbage companies. At first he did it "on the side" while still running the garbage company. In this way he did save some money for his security pad. In the end he sold his businesses to the garbage company and went back to work for them, which really wasn't any change. He still drove the same pick-up from the same home back to the garbage company instead of to his shop, which was only ten blocks away. But Stan did learn a sincere respect for business operators, and the risks that they have to endure.

These extra work endeavors did cost him two marriages. Stan holds no regret, because he wouldn't have his current wife if either the others had survived, but Stan did understand that they wanted a husband at home, not a workaholic.

So like always, Stan won't tell you what to do. If you have an idea, and have penciled out a financial plan that is realistic, Stan will give you his enthusiastic support. Stan didn't fail in business, although he did fail in two marriages. It just was not for Stan. That doesn't mean that it won't be for you. As Stan reflects, he has always had a strong connection with his bosses, almost a "winning team" atmosphere. Stan found that running his own business was, well, lonely, both at work and at home. Stan has not found that "being the boss" was all that great.

E: Family. Stan does not have to concern himself with family money, because there just is none. It's the same for his wife. What they inherited was some old junk knick knacks, guns, and pets. There was no family fortune. Stan reflects that it is just as well. All he has ever seen from family money is squabbles, and some losers that won't work. STAN SAYS: "too much money screws people up!" and he believes that based on his experiences. Nobody that Stan knows that inherited any significant amount of money has shown to him that their priorities in life are anything that Stan would want to emulate. Don't misunderstand; Stan likes to spend money. He'd be fine if a pile of money fell in his lap with no strings attached.

At first he would pay off all of his bills. Then he would travel, after he got tired of that, a couple months, Stan would seek out ways to do good in society with the money. Not dole it out to folks, but set up a self-sustaining trust to be worked out of by sincere people. This could be medical care, or waste reduction, or partner to create energy from landfill gases. None of this would be reinventing the wheel, just finding sincere efforts to support.

Stan has an old cuckoo clock that he inherited. It was in his entire childhood, and old family photos show it on the wall in the background. This clock was in a box in the cat room in the barn for thirty years because it never did work right, Stan's dad would fiddle with the thing, and cuss it. Eventually it would fall six feet to the floor with a loud "CLANG" that Stan will never forget followed by a solid half hour of cussing. Stan dug it out one day and his wife took the cuckoo clock challenge; she was going to fix the damn thing. After several months, several "CLANGS" and some more cussing, she found "the cuckooclockologist". They packed the clock up and sent it twenty five hundred miles. Upon inspection the cuckooclockologist announced the poor thing was so damaged from falling off the wall that it was not worth fixing; that they could buy a new one cheaper. Stan wanted his clock fixed, and didn't care about the damage or cost. The cuckooclockologist put a new works mechanism, from Germany, into the clock and sent it back. When Stan opened the box he saw the new weights, which were shaped like pine cones.

Stan called the cuckooclockologist and asked why he replaced the original weights. His response was that the weights were the wrong ones. The weights that Stan had were for a different clock, and these are the correct weight for Stan's clock. Stan's wife listened to the clock. Every half hour there was one "CLANG" for the half hour, and every hour there were as many "CLANGS" and the bird comes out and cuckoo's how every many times the hour is. After day one she said "why would anyone want one of those damn things in their house?" Now she can't sleep without hearing it.

So Stan reflects of course. He wonders if his dad is watching from "beyond" somewhere. Notice Stan didn't suggest "below", because his dad was well intended, just like Archie Bunker. But he fought that clock from day one when they bought it, with weights that were too light to make it work properly. Stan laughs at the situation as he enjoys his clock. He has it mounted on the wall right behind his recliner and fusses with the thing nonstop. He smiles, because it keeps near perfect time, and all the fussing fidgeting and "CLANGS" that he heard, literally all of his childhood. STAN SAYS: "the only ones that'll screw ya is your friends and family, because you won't let anybody else".

So what you got from Stan for family money is a cuckoo clock story because that's the sum total of Stan's life experiences. Stan used a three inch lag screw and mounted his cuckoo clock into corner studs at his living room. It would take a passenger jet or semi through the house to cause it to fall to the floor. This is typical of Stan and his wife. They put money into things that nobody would want, usually for sentimental reasons. They are grateful that they can. Once Stan gets his property paid off he will have met his financial goal. He has enough in his 401k to pay it off, so he is calm about it. Practically, he needs to balance his interest deduction to their annual incomes for tax purposes, so he is in no rush. Stan reflects. Because his property is forty acres they could not obtain a conventional home loan. This is similar to what the Indians have with allotment land. Stan has been in foreign countries where there is no, or little middle class. Therefore, only the rich that don't need it can get financing. Stan could not obtain a home loan to build a new house, even though he and his wife both have nice houses currently. Stan had to get a "farm" loan. He had never experienced this. He has bought at least six houses in his life. The reason he could not get a conventional home loan is because lenders feel that they cannot foreclose profitably on any parcel over five acres. It was considered a "farm". So Stan pursued a "farm" loan. It was an interesting experience for him, even though he has executed multimillion dollar transactions in the garbage trade. Basically, he already had a farm loan "to buy the farm", literally. What they wanted was a loan to build the new house, on the farm land. He had records to show that he actively farmed the forty acres; Irrigation, equipment, hay sales. What they required was a debt to income ratio of less than thirty percent. Stan had to figure this out. Nobody that he knew had a debt ratio of less than thirty percent to their income, including a nice house. Stan had a new tractor and barn, at least two hundred thousand dollars in collateral. So Stan and his wife sold both of their houses and lived in their barn while they built their new house. Yes it sucked for a while. The cats liked it. But Stan now understands what it is like not to qualify for a home loan even though you have almost a million dollars in equity. Stan reflects that it is the same for the Indians. They can't get financing on their land because lenders cannot foreclose on tribal land. Stan highly recommends the thirty percent maximum debt to income ratio. Your life is much less stressful, and you learn to adjust to the financial freedom, but you have to be disciplined. Once you have the farm loan it's easy to run out and buy a new car, or furniture, or other items that blow your debt to income ratio.

Stan's concern is leaving his family debt. He realizes that he could "have the big one" any time, and simply not wake up. He has expressed his concerns so much that everybody is sick of hearing it. He and his wife have actually out lived a couple wills, because things change over time, and feel that it is time to do another one. Just like the Business section, STAN SAYS: "plan your work, and work your plan. The Indian Elders say "you don't schedule death, it's always an unplanned surprise".

F: Bankruptcy. Stan has no personal experience in this, other than having to pick up someone's garbage that did not pay him, and filed bankruptcy. It is as if the prior account had never existed, and they start out fresh with a clean slate. It is a bitter pill to swallow, as Stan already had to pay the driver, dump fee, equipment vendor, and fuel guy. Stan does not like it, but he accepts it just as he does the state law on divorces. There are some advantages. First, since Stan's garbage company is a State regulated monopoly, all of the expenses go into Stan's rate filing, so he shares the bad debt somewhat with the new account. This account actually helped Stan get a rate increase. In another backwards plus, Stan can no longer pursue debt collection through a credit bureau, commonly referred to as a collection agency, so he stops throwing money and effort down that hole. As Stan looks at all the outstanding balances every billing cycle, he is sure to stop accounts that get too deep, say in over one hundred dollars over thirty days.

Stan's nasty attorney that coached him through his second divorce actually advised that Stan file bankruptcy following his divorce. Stan could not stiff honest businesses, it was not their fault. Sure it was legal, and it would make a very clear break from the ex, but Stan just sucked it up, paid off two trucks and two horse trailers, actually with half of her 401k. He ate a lot of grilled cheese and tomato soup. He closed all joint accounts, set up his own new, and filed an individual tax return. In a year he was back where he started, mostly due to a housing market that fell his way.

So Stan does not have a recommendation. As always, search your heart for what you hold close. It may be the correct course for you. It was not for Stan.

Stan was in the throes of his second divorce when he broke his brain. Actually, he was double covered above his insurance plan because he was also on his wife's plan, and no one could cancel anyone until the divorce was final, which was after Stan had gone home. If he had not been double covered the medical bills may have forced bankruptcy as the claim exceeded one million dollars.

Stan has seen people that start a business, run up the

bills, file bankruptcy, and do it again. That's not hard to track in a small town. Stan has never heard of an Indian filing bankruptcy. They have their own tribal court, and his collection agency had to file through the tribal court, but he can't actually recall an Indian that filed bankruptcy. Stan just doesn't know how this works. None of Stan's Indian customers would have been into him over fifty bucks, so it was not as big of a deal as a construction contractor that builds new homes, or refurbishes existing houses.

So bankruptcy is here only as a legal option in some cases. STAN SAYS: "just because it's legal doesn't make it right". Stan literally worked his way out of his financial difficulties, and suggests that it is possible for you to as well.

RELATIONSHIPS

A: Love. STAN SAYS: "if I could control love, I wouldn't take other people's garbage for a living". But Stan recognizes love, and what he has, again from lessons learned the hard way. Stan won't tell you what to do, or how to do it. STAN SAYS: "there's a reason I've been married three times".

Stan's first suggestion is to reflect on what you hold in your heart. There are multiple thresholds of love; love of family, love of country, love of religion, love of money, love of music, love of art, love of job or career, love of science, love of animals. Stan reflects that love is something that cannot be defined by any expression of boundaries, but by something that you hold in your heart that cannot be explained.

Stan reflects that people change over time. Stan has

seen it in the juvenile court system that he volunteered for. The "bad" kids did not necessarily have bad parents. Often they were simply influenced by other kids that made an impression on them, for whatever reason. The only thing the parents were guilty of was trusting their child too much, and allowing them unsupervised "freedom". But Stan realizes that he is not the same person that he was before he broke his brain, and he is not the same person he was thirty years ago, nor forty five years ago. Beyond that, he would not go back to his previous lives.

Stan reflects on his marriages, all three of them. Generally, people change over time. You are not the same person at thirty that you were at seventeen. Stan was young, had just turned twenty one at his first marriage, to a gal he dated for four years in a small town. He was divorced at twenty eight. People call it "the seven year itch" which seems to be the case as often as not. There were no children in this first marriage, so the sheets were split, along with the assets, and everyone moved on in their lives. STAN SAYS: "easy peasy lemon squeezy". But in that seven years Stan totally changed. He was transferred to larger companies as a supervisor. They moved to different cities twice, and she gave up her jobs and school. He started his own fabrication company. He worked twelve hours a day, seven days a week. No wonder she dumped him for a coworker; "fricken garbage man".

Stan was a bachelor for another seven years. His ex-wife actually tried to get him back, God knows why, and made a dramatic scene at Stan's father's graveside funeral service that would have made Archie Bunker proud. Stan had been literally on the road, internationally, with his first owner. When he returned stateside he went to work for his second owner, which was introduced from the first owner. That job lasted twenty years.

Stan dated his next wife, who was also an RN. His father died. She had a small boy from a previous marriage, and they wed, then had a baby girl. This lasted closer to twelve years, so Stan can neither confirm nor deny the seven year itch philosophy. It probably should have ended sooner. Both had changed, and Stan still worked mega hours at the garbage company, but they tried to stay together so the kids would "have a family".

Stan has reflected that all people change, and some actually "grow" together. Stan has reflected that his weddings' didn't last a lifetime, even though everyone promised God "until death do we part". Stan is grateful that his two former marriage's dissolved. He doesn't like the phrase "amicably" but there were no shots fired.

Stan would not have met his current wife if he was still in one of the other marriages. As Stan reflects this, and discusses it with his wife, he wonders how they would have got along, and if they would still be married, if she had been the first wife all those years ago, when Stan was a different person. They both agree, probably not. Both are strong willed and a little stubborn. They both liked the same things and have similar childhoods.

They understand and accept each other. Nobody else gets them, not even their siblings. Each allows the other their "freedom" but neither takes advantage of that. They both support each other's desires.

So as Stan reflects love, he has come to understand that he truly loves his wife, above everything else, even his life. He desires that they always be together. They both think "that they will be the first to go" even though Stan is several years older. But she has a history of heart disease in her family. Stan's family has either died young from self-inflicted health issues, or lived to be ancient. Both are in good health now, but have accepted mortality, however that may occur. STAN SAYS: "putting a known carcinogen in your mouth and lighting it on fire ain't smart".

Stan's wife has two grown daughters, and Stan has one, a senior in college. They fret over all three, but in reality they are exactly where they want them to be. Stan desires that all three have fulfilling lives, and find contentment. Americans are again lucky in that everyone is free. Stan realizes that is not the case for young women in other parts of the world.

Stan's wife's youngest daughter has two children. Stan enjoys this immensely. Baylee is a seven year old girl, and is the spitting image of her grandmother, right down to the left hand dominance. Everything; the way she casts her gaze, her body posture, her attitude. Stan calls her "mini me" as in the Austin Powers movie. But it gives

Stan the opportunity to observe his wife when she was that age – STUBBORN. As an example, when she wants to go somewhere she just raises her left elbow and pushes her way through with an "SKUZE ME" as she shoves you aside. Stan can't wait for the teenage years, and how those evolve. Everyone else is dreading it.

Stan's view on relationships has to include work. By Stan's math you spend eight hours a day at work, eight hours at home, and eight hours asleep. Stan and his wife use the term "work wives" because you spend as much waking time with a coworker as you do your spouse. Stan reflects that is one reason his businesses didn't thrive. They made money okay, but Stan needs a supervisor that he bonds with. Not someone to tell him what to do. Stan is self-directing. But he needs a friend that is at least at his level, or above, that supports his wacky schemes. Stan needs to trust his boss, and that they've got his back. This is not the corporate world. Stan has that with the Indians, even though he is not Indian.

There are other relationships beyond spouse, children, family, and work. A big one for Stan is his animals. He jokes that he's had some of his horses longer than he has been married, which is funny, except Stan knows that he will have to put them down soon. This breaks Stan's heart, but he understands it. He does it himself, with love.

Stan is at the point in his life where he has to look up an old business acquaintance, from maybe fifteen or twenty years ago. As often as not the person was older than Stan. The telephone conversation always begins the same; the receptionist answers and Stan asks "is Ron still alive?" If the receptionist laughs that's a yes, if she asks "who's Ron" that's probably a no. Stan wishes them peace and contentment.

B: Work. That's right, work is in Stan's relationships world. As stated previously, if you are gainfully employed, you spend as many waking hours with your coworkers as you do with your family. If you are running your company, then your work relationships extend from your coworkers to your vendors people, and your customers, as well as the bank, insurance company, and on and on. Stan's wife refers to these work relationships as "your work wife" which does share some parallels.

As an example we will use Stan's fuel vendor, Garth. Sian has a ten thousand gallon fuel tank. Garth's truck and trailer combination can haul eight thousand five hundred gallons of number two diesel legally. Stan's garbage company uses one thousand gallons of diesel, on average, every day, five days a week. Tuesday might be nine hundred ninety gallons, but Friday is one thousand ten gallons. Garth has told Stan that he is his best customer, and that he appreciates the business. Stan has questioned the local construction companies and the school districts use. Garth said yes, those are very good customers, but Stan is the only one that is consistent week to week, all year around; that the construction company doesn't run in the winter, and the school buses don't run in the summer. Garth and Stan have built a relationship based on mutual needs, and trust. Stan gets the very best pricing because he pays the bill within ten days of being invoiced. Garth does not have "to bank" the fuel loads. Of course all of Garths competitors want Stan's business, and promise the moon.

They work together closely. Garth has several generations of family savvy in the fuel industry. Stan knows garbage trucks. There is only a one day window that Stan's tank can accept a full load of Garth's fuel. Garth has a key to the gate so he can access the tank to off-load at night after the garbage trucks have fueled. Stan has learned a lot from Garth, intuitively. How you can predict price changes, up or down, based on media reports in the Middle East, whether Congress is in session or not, national elections, hurricanes, tornadoes and other events around this country, or the world, that have absolutely nothing to do with Stan's garbage company. Garth would give Stan a call and warn that the price of number two diesel would go up or down in a day or two, or "market reactions". Stan would agree to take a load, even though there wasn't yet room in his tank. Garth would park the loaded truck, and deliver it whenever the tank was below eighty five hundred gallons.

They did this for many years. Stan never ran out of fuel, even though he only had a one day window, and mountain passes in winter came into play. They developed a mutual trust based on the others performance. If a month happened to have three fuel deliveries fall in the 4.33 weeks (52 weeks/12 months = 4.33 weeks per month) it would generate a sixty thousand dollar fuel bill for one month. There were no kickbacks or pro sports tickets, as Garth's competitors offered, Stan was squeaky clean in regards to any audit.

Garth told Stan that his account was what he based his employee's medical insurance, retirement, and other benefits on. It was the only account that Garth had that was big enough, and consistent enough, to cover those costs year around. Now Stan had not only his employee's welfare to worry about, he had Garth's employees as well.

Stan would ask you to reflect on your operation's effect on the local community. It is far more than "buying local." There are no oil wells or refineries in Stan's county, so none of this diesel was "local". But Stan's garbage company supported a local business that had a little league coach and a Bluebird leader, and car show enthusiasts. STAN

SAYS: "everybody knows somebody, and that somebody knows somebody. That is the definition of community".

In some way or another all of Stan's life experiences involve his work, and math. As stated previously, Stan's Italian descendent owner had him "load" his allowed expenses every five to seven years with new equipment, and then "lean" the company out for the next several years before they would do it again.

Stan was so in-tune to his fuel consumption that he actually knew which truck used how many gallons on a given route day. Some routes have hills, others are flat. Stan also "spec'd" the new trucks that they ordered. When he received a new garbage truck he tracked the reduction in fuel consumed. Often the more modern equipment used ten percent less fuel. That's about five thousand a month, or sixty thousand a year (250,000 gallons X $2.50 per X .10 = $62,500). This fuel savings was a driver's salary for a year. Stan was never shorthanded. STAN SAYS: 'when you do the work yourself you get it your way".

So reflect on all of your relationships, even the ones that you may not consider a relationship. If there are people involved, it's a relationship. As you reflect, is this someone that you would "want to be in bed with?" Rhetorically of course. If not, make a change. Not everything is a bargain. Sometimes spending more is the better value. STAN SAYS: "there's two prices, the high price and the higher price. I only want to pay the high price".

C: The Broken Heart. Once again, Stan will not tell you what to do. This is a very deep, complicated subject, and is different for every heart involved. There is no straight arrow, no sure path to follow. Of course Stan reflects. He has learned what not to do, with his heart. Stan is not making light of a complicated issue that varies from one person to the next. As Stan reflects, he has come to realize that "his style" is to make something humorous out of a very sad situation. To begin, the only people that can break your heart are the people that you let in, usually friends or family. That is because you won't allow anyone else to break your heart. Basically, they let you down, or disappointed you. When Ashley stole the early pregnancy test kit from the store, and took it into the store restroom, used it with "a positive result", she disappointed her parents, and had some heady issues to deal with. But that does not mean that she broke her parent's hearts. Either of them might feel that she did, but she did not engage in unprotected sex out of wedlock to disappoint her parents. That was not her intention. That was not "in her heart", just like her mother did not break her father's heart by not "making sure that everything was covered" like it falls on the mother alone to school the daughter about birth control by age twelve,

So if either parent feels that Ashley broke their heart, that is their individual feeling, for their reasons, not Ashley's. The true test of love will be how all three deal with this situation moving forward. Couples deal with this all of the time for various reasons. There are jealousies, both real and imagined. There are histories on both sides. Stan does suggest "opening you heart" which sounds very noble, but frankly, is dangerous. When you open your heart you risk getting it broken. Stan opens his anyway. Stan has had a lot of disappointment in his life. He has been betrayed time and time again. STAN SAYS: "those lessons you learn the hard way are the ones that you remember".

Stan has had a few surgeries in his life. Remember, Stan does not like pain medication He prefers the pain to the drugs. When asked about his pain by a doctor or nurse STAN SAYS: "I've had broken hearts that hurt worse".

When Stan has been betrayed, the instinct was to react, but Stan reflects on his reaction. Basically, once someone has betrayed Stan's trust, he closes the "circle of trust:", and that person is not allowed back in. They may ask forgiveness, which Stan gives freely, but they are not allowed back in the circle, ever. Remember Stan lives his life by "give them the benefit of the doubt until they give you a reason not to". This is a recipe for disaster, admittedly, but a lot of Stan's positive life experiences have come from "wearing his heart on his sleeve."

When these folks reappear in Stan's life behaving like nothing happened, just like the unarmed man in a battle of wits, STAN SAYS: "please don't take any more of my heartbeats that I'll never get back", followed by "in a lot of cultures they consider that murder". Then count "one potato, two potato…" There ya go! If that does not make your point, well, you're in a battle of wits with an unarmed man. Just look them in the eye, smile knowingly, and walk away. Then let it go. Your brain is a different organ than your heart. Sure they work together, but you can operate them individually. Letting it go doesn't mean that you don't hate the dipshit mentally, but that hatred is not in your heart. Once you have experienced this freedom, you will be happy, and you heart is no longer "broken". But remember, if you open your heart, it is going to happen again, if you live long enough.

Reflect on what is in your heart. That's why Stan calls it your heart. It's yours, only you decide. You have to decide on the priorities. It's okay for those to change over time. They almost always do. Try not to hold more than two desires. Just reflect that getting severely disappointed over someone else not allowing you to control their thoughts or actions is not their fault, it's yours. Every human has the right to happiness and freedom in their life. Just smile, and breathe, and walk away. Let it go. That doesn't mean that you stop caring, you're just not allowing it to poison your heart.

Stan truly loves, and respects his wife as probably the most fantastic human being on earth. He would rather die than live without her. That does not mean that they agree on everything, they do not. They just allow the other person to be what they are, without judgment.

Stan has experienced that raising children is frightening. You never stop worrying about "what if". Stan has reflected that the best you can do is be honest and approachable about anything when they come to you with any problem or need, and just let them make their mistakes in life. Even though they may be "informed mistakes", understand that everyone makes mistakes. The uptick is that they are coming to you.

So Stan understands the heartbreak. He accepts it as a fact of life if you are going to allow people in. STAN SAYS: "there are two kinds of people; those that have had their heart broken, and those that are going to". Stan does not advocate closing your heart. Stan has done this. It results in a loneliness that may be worse than the heartbreak, or maybe just a different kind of heartbreak, but just as painful. Open your heart, accept that it will get broken, learn from the experience, and move on. Don't be bitter, don't react, and don't "get even". Just smile, breathe, and walk away. Let it go. STAN SAYS: "bye bye now". All said and done it's your life. It is not up to others to "make" you be happy and content

D: The Break-up. As all things in life, this can be multifaceted. The break-up could be getting fired, quitting, or laid off from a job that started with high expectations, on both ends. It could be a divorce, which again started with high expectations. It could be a friendship soured for some slight. It could be family. If you have adopted desires that you hold in your heart, you can navigate these break-up's pretty well. No one gets married to be divorced, or hires a contractor to build a substandard house. We'll use Stan's fuel vendor as the example, since that's recent, and well thought through. This was a twenty year relationship built on trust; each party holding up their end. These were not "social" friends. They never went out to dinner or had a beer together. They both had daughters the same age, in different school districts. So they would sit next to each other and cheer for opposite teams at the girl's high school basketball game. Whoever's team lost congratulated the other man.

Stan was "heartbroken" when he had to tell Garth that they would no longer be buying fuel from them; that the national company that bought them engaged in "futures" trading, so Stan would be buying on a national account paying five to ten percent more. Garth was unemotional, and if he had any response, it was a smile. Garth told Stan "don't worry about it. I've been expecting this. Thank you for telling me in person. If there's ever anything I can do for you, let me know". This was a valuable life lesson that Stan would never forget.

When you get to the divorce of a marriage, there are so many variables. Stan has been though it enough that he doesn't get caught up in "the wind-up". Basically, all of this crap is a matter of law based on the state that you reside in. No, the state of denial is not a state. The Nile is a river. So how the assets get split, the equity value of the house owed to whoever got the boot, the split of the retirement accounts, even social security, are a matter of law by state. Getting that nasty high priced attorney that "kick's ass" may make you feel better, but the only one that will get more money is them.

When it comes to any dependent (less than eighteen years old) children, this is a time to reflect. What is in their best interest? Who is the better parent? Of course who gets custody will determine child support payments;

But Stan reckons that's cheap compared to actually raising the child. If you reflect, you may come to the decision that it is in the child's best interest to live with the other parent. Of course age plays a big part in the decision process. A six month old that gets moved from Seattle to Jacksonville probably wouldn't notice, but a sixteen year old that is first violin in the orchestra, and her grandfather is her coach, may be a different matter.

There's always extenuating circumstances. The person you thought you knew decided that they were gay, or the garbage man is in better physical shape, and makes more money. Then there's the pets, cars, Knick knacks, blah, blah, blah.

Generally, if it is something you held prior to the sacred vows, you retain it, like a horse or a dog. In some states the child has a say if they are over sixteen. This is a wake-up call for a lot of folk's. It is not uncommon to have your ex dump your kid at your place "before they have to kill 'em". Stan recognizes that this contact can be dangerous. Of course both parents love their kids and want the best for them. But these interactions have led to problems. Both of Stan's ex-wives wanted him back, after they realized that the grass really wasn't that much greener. Really? Do you want to be back with someone that gave you the boot, showed you the door, and hired the nasty attorney?

In regards to the nasty attorney, as stated, you are only allowed what the law allows. It does not matter how nasty the attorney is. There are all kinds of relationships. What Stan has learned is that it is common for the opposing attorneys to play a round of golf, have a drink or two with lunch at the country club, and scheme on how to fan the flames of emotion to bill more hours at $200 plus per hour.

Here's what Stan does. He's not telling you what to do, just what he does. He uses your ex's attorney for the divorce. That's right, no typo. Then he hire's his own nasty attorney to coach him on the law. The first attorney cannot take both parties if there is any disagreement. So Stan goes into the meetings with what the law allows. When his ex makes a demand, and that is within the law, he gives it to her. She really thinks that she kicked his ass. Most of her "legal advice" was coming from a bunch of divorced boozers warming bar stools, so it didn't require a high IQ.

Of course the attorney recognized what he was up to, and threw out a couple bones to pick over. Stan knew what was allowed, and just admittedly gave it to her. Stan always has a back-up plan. He would meet with "his attorney" to discuss the issues. If the arrangement ever fell apart he would have his own nasty attorney on board that could step right in. Stan's attorney counseled bankruptcy once the divorce was final. Stan, again the business mind, could not stiff anyone that he promised to pay buying a car, horse trailer, whatever. His wife ran all the credit cards up, but once they were separated, those bills were hers. Stan opened his own bank account, and fed the kids out of a piggy bank he had rat holed for many years. There was a lot of grilled cheese sandwiches and tomato soup.

So Stan's soon to be ex-wife hires the nasty attorney her barstool coaches suggested. He banged off a form letter demanding tax returns, W-2 forms, and all the stuff that is a part of the law in Stan's state. When she came to the house to collect a saddle, and see the kids, she was very belligerent; basically telling Stan her "new" attorney would be kicking his ass. Stan reflected, and explained that no, that wasn't how it was going to go. The way it was going to go was if they agreed on the divorce, each would get half, including custody. If she wanted to fight, the nasty attorney would get all the money, he and she would get zero, she would probably have the kid's full time, and both would have to file bankruptcy and give up their vehicles. She went back to her original attorney.

E: Termination of Employment. Once again this topic has been moved around, the latest move from Finances, for obvious reasons. Like all topics involved in this collection of musings, they all fall under Life. Indeed your employment is a relationship, entered into on both sides with high hopes and expectations, just like a wedding. As stated you spend one third of your waking life at your job with your coworkers, just like with your family. Stan always held the view that your job should be your third priority in your life. Number one should be your family, number two should be your home, where your family is safe, and your job supports the first two.

Stan has experienced both sides of separation of employment. He has been hired, with expectations; he has quit, usually going to another job. He has been fired or laid off. In all of these serious life changes, Stan reflects that each one was a benefit to both parties. Indeed, Stan's life has always improved in quality, if not financial, by all of his separations of employment. Stan has also had to terminate other's employment. Stan takes this very seriously. They are never taken by surprise. He talks to everyone and they know the expectations, so Stan informs them that if they don't live up to the expectations, which are not excessive, you are in essence, firing yourself.

The examples are varied as much as people are. Some are for failing a DOT mandated drug test. With these there are no warnings, but nobody can act surprised by a positive result. Dr Judy has consulted Stan on the results as she is their MRO (Medical Review Officer) for the DOT panels. Stan doesn't know anyone that can eat that many poppy seed muffins, but he does the dance. Some are for accidents. Stan is sending twenty five ton machines into folk's neighborhoods around their children, pets, and homes, every day. He takes this responsibility very seriously, literally life and death.

Stan has had occurrences where one of his route drivers "sets up his own route" in which he takes cash payments from folks for picking up their trash outside of the company billing. Stan has an unorthodox way of watching for this. STAN SAYS: "you can tell a lot about a garbage company by the employee parking lot". Benny taught him this lesson. He paid cash for a brand new four wheel drive pick-up with the six hundred and forty shoes that he returned to the high end store. STAN SAYS: "everything you need to know will come in by phone".

Stan would send an employee out "blind" to cover routes for illnesses or vacation coverage. They did not know the route, and did not ride along prior to. They had to pick up the route off of the route sheet, which in a convoluted way is a billing statement. No account on the route sheet, leave the cans. Stan let his CSR's know that he wanted to take any calls for misses from that route. The folks that actually paid cash on the side would call in when their garbage was missed! Stan would go to the home, take the lid off, and often there was a ten dollar bill and a can of beer on top of the trash. When he went to the door Stan would ask "how long we been pickin' up your garbage?" The person would answer something like "I've been a customer for three years." Stan would say "thank you, we'll back bill you and once your account is current we'll pick up your trash" to a dumfounded look. They would have a new driver the next week.

San would also just grab some invoices randomly out of the billing every month. We're talking five invoices' out of forty thousand. He would call, or visit the customer and discuss their garbage service. Stan gave a lot of drivers one hundred dollars, out of his own pocket, and Friday off as a thank you. STAN SAYS: "when you do everything yourself you get it your way", and "I can do any route, but I can't do every route."

Many of the calls that the CSR's forwarded to Stan were not requested. He always wanted the freaks or the threatening calls. One day he got a call from the high rent district that never leaves a Christmas gift; "I don't want any goddamned Mexicans on my route!" Stan heard him out without interruption. Stan actually just laid the phone on his desk and let the idiot yell while he processed paperwork. When the guy, whom Stan reckoned was drunk, came up for air, Stan informed him that his driver was a valued employee, one of the best of sixty four drivers, and he would not be taken off the route. "I want him fired!" "That is not going to happen sir", followed by "our service is not mandatory". Silence. Then "if I quit he's still in my neighborhood!" Stan would reply "that's correct sir, unless of course, you move." The idiot would slur "who's your boss?" and Stan would reply "that's on a need to know basis" and then nothing further. Usually he was hung up on. Stan would warn the driver to be cautious of the racist. Don't confront him or even have a conversation, just dump his trash until he's an SNP (stop for nonpayment).

There was an opposite racist effect from this. "Luis" was a third generation "Mexican". He was actually of Guatemalan decent. His grandparents had been illegal's some forty years ago. Both of his parents were born in the United States, so they were legal citizens, and their children "were legal". On one occasion Stan was talking to a parts delivery driver that had broken English in the parking lot. Luis walked by and Stan asked him to interpret the conversation. "Luis looked offended and said "I don't speak wetback". Stan was taken aback. As

Stan reflected he came to realize that it was his fault, that he had assumed Luis spoke Spanish. Stan did apologize later. Luis explained that none of the third generation immigrants ever speak Spanish, that they are embarrassed by their heritage, that it stems from grade school.

One day Stan was sitting at his desk and a CSR walked in the room. She was visibly upset, shaking. Stan took the call, and yet another drunk was yelling. His garbage service had been stopped because he hadn't paid his bill, and the CSR had already explained that. Again there was no surprise, he had already been mailed two invoices, then two delinquent notices, then a notice that he would be sent to a collection agency. "Did you get the notices sir, maybe we have the wrong billing address", which does happen with post office boxes. The man confirmed that his billing address was correct. "Well sir, just so you understand, your account will be sent to a collection agency on the date on the notice." The man flew into a rage that the CSR could hear through the receiver at Stan's ear. "I'm gonna bring my shotgun down there and blow your brains out!" Stan informed the man very casually that he was welcome to come down, but that he "should stop by a pawn shop, pawn his shotgun, and pay his garbage bill." The man was silent. Then STAN SAYS: "if you don't pay the garbage bill the service gets really bad" and "if it wasn't illegal I'd bring your garbage back to you". The CSR thanked Stan for taking the call and asked if she should call the sheriff? Stan told her no, this guy had vented, and he would be harmless. About thirty minutes later the CSR walks back in with a big white man around fifty years old. She introduced him to Stan. Stan asked how we could help him? It was the shotgun idiot. He had taken Stan's advice, pawned his gun, and was here to pay his bill. STAN SAID: "I'll go pick up your garbage myself" and did, right then.

So you have unorthodox relationships that you don't even know about. Some involve race, some money, some work, some religion, you just never know, but do not assume that you do. Reflect on everything.

As Stan reflects he realizes that he is as bad as anyone else. Sometimes people talk, just to hear themselves talk, or "sound" educated. Sometimes the attempt is to make themselves look good by making others look bad. This is common in the work relationship. So Stan suggests that you just consider your words or actions before you engage in them, and all of the possibilities. Do you really need to speak, as if answering a question? If not, just smile, and breathe. There's no rush to make a jackass out of yourself.

Stan has learned, of course the hard way, that people of races other than his own are racist. Stan had always "assumed" that races other than Caucasian were not racist. Upon reflection he has no idea where that assumption came from, may be just his sensitivity to political correctness. But just because you don't use a slur to describe someone of another race does not mean that person does not use that same slur to describe others.

Stan really hasn't experienced racism directed at him. He has worked in Detroit and Atlanta, so he has been around other races in a work environment. Stan's Scottish ancestry doesn't appear to attract much notice. Stan does see it some from the Indians. You either are an Indian, or you're not. Stan has a lot of friends that he trusts that are Indians, but he has learned that you either are one of them, or you're not. Stan's okay with that; "their loss."

Stan worries about the racial atrocities' that he knows are going on all over the world. Stan leans towards being an isolationist, like a lot of the Indians do, but Stan has witnessed firsthand how the economies of several countries hinge on compromise. Stan feels that the United States just should not, and cannot, be the world police force. There are no other countries in the financial position to address all of the issues. The United Nations is a good concept, but the United States is expected to lead, and of course finance, any wrongs that are committed on the planet. Stan knows that everything does not get addressed, and the ones that are aren't done properly.

This is what fuels terrorist operations. If your life is so terrible, and there is no way to climb out of that hole, blowing yourself up in a car or plane bomb killing someone else may be the only option available to a twenty five year old (fill in the blank). Several religious faiths plays a role in this, and that mentality goes back thousands of years. Indeed, many groups consider that the "Armageddon" has already begun.

So Stan suggests that you reflect, and consider your words and actions effect on others. Don't hide from interaction with others unlike you. In fact Stan suggests "immersion". If you have a group of peoples that you fear, immerse yourself in them. You will grow as a person, and lose your fear. That is not to say you will agree with them, but you will understand their culture. Stan has seen immersion programs such as a month with a family in Costa Rica. You pay five thousand dollars, and live with a family there for one month. You are only around Spanish. You have a simple job, such as a box-boy in a grocery store. Your salary goes to the family. You share in their day to day lives, meals, media, religion, everything. In one month you are fluent in Spanish, and have a new family.

Stan reflects that this is good for those that talk too much, because nobody will know what you're saying, and you cannot understand them, at least in the first week. All you can do is observe them, and then emulate their actions. Too few people observe before they act. It doesn't need to be in a foreign language. Stan has worked in both Britain and Germany. He couldn't understand either in the beginning. Even though the British spoke the same language as Stan, and could roughly understand him, the Germans were actually easier to adjust to, in German.

F. The Grown Child. Blink! This just happens one day. All of a sudden your little pride and joy is their own person. Of course there are legal definitions by age, active in the military, married, or other dependency issues, but Stan reckons none of those apply. Stan reflects that it is what you hold in your heart. Stan recognized that his daughter was her own person when she was about fifteen, even though he still had to drive her to school, feed her, clothe her, and all the other parental responsibilities. But she made her own decisions of right and wrong. She decided what was acceptable based on her criteria.

Stan had exposed her to a Christian church some. It was the services held at the same daycare that she had gone to as a child. She was in Sunday school, and decided her own path in regards to faith. She went to the usual sorority school societal functions when she first went off to college. Stan did not intervene, but he was glad when she moved into a place of her own. She has a part time job and gets good grades. She had a steady boyfriend, but broke that off for her own reasons. Stan does not get nosey. He knows that she has a good head on her shoulders, and a good heart. It is similar for Stan's wife's daughters. They are somewhat older. One is married with two children, and one is divorced. Stan and his wife are proud of their children. All there are "grown up", even though Stan recognizes that problems can always come up. STAN SAYS "the problems don't go away, they just get bigger", but he is referring to the unruly teenage years in high school. Stan and his wife are very happy all of their children are happy, and wish a content life to all of them. They do make them make their own way in life, there are few handouts, but they help where they can. Their children recognize that their life is their responsibility, and don't ask. Both sides recognize that their parent is unconventional, and are happy that their parent found someone compatible, and are happy too.

Of course all the kids got drug through all the divorces, but as Stan reflects on his daughter, he has come to realize that she used that as an experience of what not to do, which is Stan's skill in life. Stan knows that there are things that he doesn't know about, and that's fine. Any secrets that she may have are her secrets, and up to her.

There are the usual generational differences. She cannot go five seconds without looking at her I phone, and Stan has to call his I phone with his flip phone to find it. It's usually in "the other" pair of bib overalls.

Stan reflects on when he became "independent". It was about the same age, around fifteen years old. Stan still lived at home with his dad, but he was making his own life decisions moving forward.

EPILOGUE

Well, if you've made it this far, you have enough one liners to make a dozen ten-packs of witty T-shirts, or adorn every car in the parking lot with bumper stickers that should attract a lot of key scratches. STAN SAYS: "never lose your sense of humor".

As you have that heart to heart talk with that naked dude in the mirror, realize that there are no wrong stands on an issue. It does not matter what other people think. It is not your responsibility to "make" them be happy. The only thing that matters is what you hold in your heart as your desires. It's okay if they change over time, in fact, expect them to. There are times with no children, then times of raising children, then no children again. Your desires can change as your life changes. The only thing that matters is what your desires are, right now, today.

Try not to hold too many desires. The Buddhist monks suggest a maximum of two, or they tend to cancel each other out, and you get frustrated, and fail. Some folks have success with resolutions, or promises to themselves. Some get mental support from religion, others from politics, or service clubs, or associations that address issues. Whatever works for you. Try not to let anyone control you to be accepted. Just be yourself, true only to yourself.

Practice controlling your mental faculty separate from your heart strings. This is the practice of reflecting rather than reacting. It does encompass emotions to a degree. You can dislike someone mentally without any reaction, or letting them poison your heart. The first step is older than you are; "think before you speak". Most people do not. Don't allow your reactions to draw you into what Stan calls "a stupid contest". If there is a winner of a stupid contest, what do they win? Just to be recognized as more stupid than the other stupid person? What'ya gonna do with that?

As you learn to be reflective and consider such outcomes, you will develop a relaxed demeanor in which your face relaxes, and breathing and a gentle smile become natural. It is okay to exit the area and let the other party be reactive. It does not show weakness. It exhibits intelligence, and self-control.

As you determine your desires, what you hold close to your heart, you can limit who you surround yourself with.

It should be considered a privilege to be allowed in your circle of trust. This does not mean that you close people out. Sometimes you can't, like a cashier at a business. When you get everybody, you get everybody, the good, the bad, and the ugly. But that doesn't mean that they are allowed into your personal space. No salary pays for that. You can be kind, and polite to everyone, even mean spirited people. Do not react to anything they say or do. Just smile, reflect, and breathe.

Don't allow yourself to be forced to make a decision prior to completing your reflection. This needs to be modified for safety issues like calling 911 for an emergency, but frankly, how many true emergencies do you encounter in a lifetime. It's okay to say "I need to think about it", as long as you do, and respond. It comes off a little cheap if you beg off and never do respond.

Every person on Earth has personal issues. Those are theirs, yours are yours. It is up to you if you allow theirs to be yours. It isn't complicated if that is in your heart as a desire. If it is not, you don't allow it. It's your heart. You can't buy them at a market.

So list your hearts desires. Pare it down to a couple. Then every decision that you make, every action you take, leads to the fulfillment of your desires. This may be too much change for some people. Do not compromise your desires. You can reflect on every aspect of your life. It is important to be open minded, and accepting to different points of view. It's okay to change your point of view irreguardless of what others think. It's your point of view, not theirs.

None of this works, or matters, if you don't take care of your physical body; regular exercise, eat well, sleep, fresh air. Don't close everyone out. Give people the benefit of the doubt until they give you a reason not to. Trust your instincts. If you don't like the way someone treats a critter then that's your reason not to give them the benefit of the doubt. The bottom line is it is your reason.

So this desire to take care of your body may be your first desire, and you prioritize that until you are healthy. This is not cosmetic, like Botox injections or hair implants. It does include any dental work until you are healthy. Once you are in good physical shape, by your definition, you will make any necessary life choice changes, and begin eating and sleeping better. You will find that you do a lot of quality reflection just prior to falling asleep, or immediately after you awaken. It is like your brain "resets" once all the stimuli is set aside. When Stan suggests good physical shape, this does not mean appearance as in hair style, wardrobe, or jewelry, everyone is beautiful on the inside.

Now the healthy you is eating and sleeping well, regularly. Your brain function is much improved for the reflection ahead of you. Of course too much alcohol or drugs affects your brain functions, and any reflections under those conditions are probably not worth acting on. You need to decide what your desires are.

As you go through your day to day, reflect on every minute detail. Does this fit in your desire? There are personal interactions, such as family and coworkers, and there is impersonal such as Face book, email, or texting. It is too easy to be reactive when you are tapping onto a piece of plastic, so Stan suggests that your serious communications be in person. That will make people outside of your circle of trust nervous. Reflect on that. Try not to be indifferent. Stan suggests that you envision a cat turning and walking away from you when you call to it with "your kitty voice". That cat doesn't give you the doggy finger at feeding time.

So as you decide who aligns with your hearts desires, there are going to be some rejects. That does not mean that you have to be rude. Stan suggests that you just treat people like you would want to be treated if the situation were reversed. Often that may simply boil down to staying away from them, and leaving them alone._There is no "getting even" in a relationship. All that you accomplish in the attempt is more "to get even" for on both sides. Just smile, breathe, and walk away.

That does not suggest that you just forget any slights that may have occurred. You do not forget. But your brain is not your heart. If you calmly reflect, you can just accept the wrong done to you was; One, a learning experience; two, a sign of the other's true character. That does not mean that you don't say good morning in the hall at work, but it does mean that you don't want to go have a cup of coffee with them. Leave the past in the past. You can't change it.

To some, the count of friends is a priority. Friendship is not a number threshold. Upon reflection you may discover that one or two friends is more enjoyable than a hundred.

Once you have your desires for this stage of your life, just be. It will all fall into place. This is not complicated. Do not be afraid to try new and different things. That will expand your reflections and desires. Accept what is acceptable to you, and reject what is not. This could mean a change in careers or relationships, but that is based on your desires in your heart. You do not compromise your desires. If they are not for somebody else, adios.

Your brain and your heart are separate organs. Yes they interact, but human beings hold the capacity to control their brain, and not allow it to poison their heart. Does your brain control your kidneys, or liver? It only affects your heart if you allow it to. That is the difference between humans and animals. Reflect rather than react.

ABOUT THE AUTHOR

Scott Robertson was born in 1957. His mother and father were each divorced from a previous marriage with three children each. Scott was the oldest of the next three. His mailing address has always been in Washington State. He was raised in an Archie Bunker type home in the All in the Family television show. That does not mean that he has not been around. Scott has worked in Europe, Canada, Mexico, and South America with non- Americans. He has experienced other types of media and news coverage. He has witnessed other government's controls over market conditions. Stan reflects that there are other countries similar to the United States, but he has not seen any "just like it".

Scott suffered a near fatal brain injury the day before he turned fifty three. In many ways he has never recovered, nor does he want to. Life is different. He does not regret any of his former life before his injury. His life was very good by American standards; home, job, income, family.

Older Americans would like the opportunity "to start over". When you shear your brain you don't get a choice, you have to start over. Most of his neurologists suggested taking up a foreign language, computer science, or art such as painting or sculpture, or some other mentally challenging task, as your brain works overdrive as you heal. This is a multi-year process.

Scott discovered that his previous life experiences came to him as he was experiencing "new" things, which were the "normal" things in his previous life. As he pondered these differences, he came to understand that most of his beliefs prior to his injury just were not important any longer, and he had adopted not "new", but different philosophies about most things in life. Some of his previous priorities remained; Family, animals, health, but he didn't care about corporate politics or what the P & L posted. He embraced "fake news" before it was a buzz word on twitter. He realized that it just doesn't matter who the president is.

Scott lives with his true love on their forty acre farm with their twenty critters, and is still a garbage man. Please enjoy his other works; Right Foot Down!, Rat A Tat Tat, and Taco!?!?!